DUPLICITY

N. K. TRAVER

DUPLICITY

THOMAS DUNNE BOOKS
ST. MARTIN'S GRIFFIN
NEW YORK

THOMAS DUNNE BOOKS.
An imprint of St. Martin's Press.

DUPLICITY. Copyright © 2015 by N. K. Traver. All rights reserved. Printed in the United States of America. For information, address St. Martin's Press, 175 Fifth Avenue, New York, N.Y. 10010.

www.thomasdunnebooks.com
www.stmartins.com

Library of Congress Cataloging-in-Publication Data

Traver, N. K.
    Duplicity / N.K. Traver.
        p. cm.
    ISBN 978-1-250-05914-7 (hardcover)
    ISBN 978-1-4668-6372-9 (e-book)
    1. Science fiction.   2. Hackers—Fiction.   3. Conduct of life—Fiction.
    4. Identity—Fiction.   5. Cloning—Fiction.   6. Love—Fiction.   I. Title.

    PZ7.1.T73Du 2015
    [Fic]—dc23   2014034092

St. Martin's Griffin books may be purchased for educational, business, or promotional use. For information on bulk purchases, please contact the Macmillan Corporate and Premium Sales Department at 1-800-221-7945, extension 5442, or write to specialmarkets@macmillan.com.

First Edition: March 2015

10   9   8   7   6   5   4   3   2   1

For Collin, who is everything I aspire to be
For my father, who taught me the value of hard work
And for my mother, who taught me to dream

DUPLICITY

1. SEVEN YEARS BAD LUCK

IT FIGURES THAT between the two of us, my laptop is the first to grow a conscience.

"You had no problem yanking credit cards last week," I remind it, tapping my finger on the desk as I glare at the words on the screen. Words that should say STARTING JOB as my newest hacking bot cracks BankPueblo.com's security layer. Words that should say PROCESSING as the bot downloads two hundred fresh account numbers to my thumb drive.

Words that should *not* say GET SOME SUNSHINE, LOSER.

I must've typed the wrong name for the bot. My laptop's full of old code I keep telling myself I'll clean out and I must've triggered one of my old insult programs. I hit the shortcut keys to close everything, then reopen the console window and type the name of the bot, again. Z-O-O-M-F-I-S-H—

ONLY COWARDS STEAL FROM THOSE WHO CAN'T FIGHT BACK, says this good-for-nothing piece of metal that dares call itself my computer.

"Yeah, yeah, I know," I mutter, but I'm not feeling so sure about this anymore. That's not an insult I would've coded into my own work. And if what's happening now isn't something I wrote . . . that means it came from somewhere else.

Which is, I remind myself, impossible.

I set my jaw and type the name of the bot. Again. All but the last letter: "zoomfis." Then I hit the H key and the Enter as fast as I can, but somehow, somehow in that millisecond between keystrokes "zoomfish" changes to PLAY A SPORT IF YOU WANT EXERCISE and I slam my fist on the desk.

How? How the hell would anyone—

My computer starts typing.

YOU SHOULD FIND A DIFFERENT HOBBY.

I didn't touch the keys. I didn't type anything that should trigger an insult, not "zoomfish," not "you freaking traitor," not anything, but there are the words on my screen, white as ice.

And my heart comes to life in my chest, because I know what this means but I want to keep thinking it's impossible.

I need to reboot. Now, before the virus digs into my hard drive and downloads my hacking bots or my passwords for the hacker forums or the list of sites I'm planning to hit after I clean out Bank Pueblo. I jab the power key to restart, but it ignores me. Ignores me and says,

YOU WEREN'T VERY NICE TO EMMA.

My blood changes direction. My fingers sting from the death grip I have on the desk, but I can't let go, can't stop shaking my head *no no no* because it can't know about that. It *can't.* That happened fifteen minutes ago, maybe twenty, and it would take longer than that to hack through the firewalls on my computer.

Which means this is more than a virus someone planted and forgot about.

Someone has a live feed to my room.

I eye the camera lens on my laptop and jerk open the desk drawer to find something to cover it. I wish I hadn't smashed the overhead light after Emma stormed out, because that leaves only my lava lamp to see by, and its useless glow is just making more shadows. My fingers find a stack of Post-its. I rip the top note off and stick it over the lens.

There are new words on the screen. Words I want to unread the second I read them.

I THINK YOU REGRET WHAT YOU SAID TO HER.

My heart thumps *Do you? Do you? Do you?* and my grip on the desk slips from sweat. Emma is none of his business. How I feel about it is none of his business. If she hadn't ruined everything telling me how she wants . . . *things* for us, I wouldn't have had to break her heart.

That weird ache starts in my gut again, the same one I almost got rid of by running zoomfish.

I don't regret things.

AFRAID OF CARING FOR SOMEONE BESIDES YOURSELF?

I'm done with this guilt trip. He's clever, I'll give him that, psyching me out while he's probably corrupted half my hard drive, and I do what I should have done to begin with and switch off the wireless. That'll kill his sicko webcam and anything he's downloading. It's going to be a pain getting the virus off my system, but—

YOU THINK IT'S THAT EASY?

I think I actually squeak. *Squeak*, like a little kid afraid of his own shadow, not someone used to living in them. I don't remember getting up but I'm five feet away from the desk now, my chair overturned in a pile of printer paper. The breath I'm holding chokes free.

He can't. He can't keep typing if I'm not connected to the Internet.

I paw for anything behind me I can use as a weapon, and I come up with—I squint in the dark—the long tube of cardboard my newest Metallica posters arrived in. Great. If something leaps out of my computer, I can amuse it to death. It'll have to do. I wait in the corner, tube poised like a bat. My laptop glows, innocent.

I inch forward.

No new messages.

I inch forward again.

The cursor blinks on and off, on and off, not typing anything. I right my chair and reach for the laptop's power cord.

YOU KNOW WHY THIS IS STILL WORKING, RIGHT?

"How the hell are you doing this?" I snarl. The tube crumples when I clench it and I chuck it aside. Nothing's going to jump out, nothing's even really happened except he's rigged the virus to type a different set of phrases after the wireless turns off. Obviously that's it. It can't be that hard to do. I'll figure out how after I dig his virus up and break it to pieces.

Then I'll find *him*.

THAT'S THE IDEA.

He just—

Did he just read my . . . ?

HERE'S THE GAME, HACKER. I'M DONE WATCHING YOU RUIN PEOPLE'S LIVES.

HEARD THE PHRASE "YOUR OWN WORST ENEMY"?

YOU'RE ABOUT TO LIVE IT.

Something in me wakes up. Common sense, maybe, because I slam the laptop closed, rip out the power cord and eject the battery, and that's what I have in my hand when I see movement to my side. I don't care if it's a moth, if he's somehow in my room I'm going to get the first move, and I chuck the battery at whatever it is and glass shatters and I duck and I realize—

I'm an idiot.

The remaining shards of my now-broken closet mirror wink at me, then drop to the floor in tattletale chimes.

I stand there a minute, breathing deep, my heart beating crazy in my ears. Something in the back of my head whispers *seven years bad luck* and something else says *that's a load of crap* and I suck a piercing in my lip, because louder than that, like the virus guy's hissing in my ear, are the words *here's the game, hacker.*

He couldn't have read my mind.

Couldn't.

I pace so I can breathe. I kick torn textbook pages and shredded posters out of the way as I go, flexing my hand, plucking splinters out of my knuckles as I glance at the fist-shaped dent in my dresser.

I remind myself I don't regret things.

I'd usually leave this mess for Mom to remind her I'm still alive, but I can't sit here waiting for my laptop to turn itself on or blow up or who knows what, so I stoop for a piece of plastic that used to be the case for an old Manson CD.

My hand is shaking and all I can do is look at it.

Because who found me? Who cares enough to find me? Can't be a cop, because he'd cut to the chase and knock on my door with a warrant, not play cat-and-mouse on my laptop. Can't be a bot because he knows personal details about me. Like what happened with Emma. But I can't think of anyone, even super hackers who get their thrills hunting other hackers, who would care what I say or do offline. Emma's not the kind of girl who'd have connections like that and she's not the kind of girl who'd get revenge, either.

Dammit, it doesn't matter what kind of girl she is. I don't need her. I don't need anyone—

Something on my floor glints. A piece of the mirror, though

I can't imagine what it's reflecting since I haven't moved. The puckish gleam of my lava lamp isn't near bright enough to cause a flash. I glance at the ceiling, at the wooden blinds half covering the window, and decide it must've been something outside. I'm tossing pieces of chapter six from my Spanish book into the trash when the shard winks again.

This time I'm focused enough to know nothing outside made that light. I pluck the glass off the floor and turn it, trying to recreate the flashing, but I get nothing. I wouldn't care except that freaking hacker guy said he wanted me to find him, didn't he? And how am I supposed to know if he means online or . . . or here? That makes me freeze and squint out the bottom of my window, but no one's shining a flashlight in, no one's standing on the street below.

I hate this. *I'm* supposed to be the kid they warn you about in those "online safety" classes. I'm supposed to be the monster, not this jerk. I'm Brandon Eriks, I like to break things, I'm good at breaking things, and if this guy's itching for a fight, he's found one. If he wants to meet, let's meet. There's a reason the kids at school stay away from me. There's a reason the Feds can't trace my hack jobs.

I just have to figure out his riddle. "Your own worst enemy. You're about to live it." They must be codes. I start working out an algorithm in my head as I pick up the rest of the shards and carry them with me to the bathroom. The phrases sound familiar, but I don't know if that's because I keep thinking them over and over or because I've seen them someplace.

I flip on the bathroom light, toss the shards into the seashell trashcan, and—and do a double take at the mirror.

No way.

It's because I'm jumpy over that whole *seven years bad luck* thing. That has to be it. I move my hand across the counter, and back. Across, back. The mirror moves with me, like a mir-ror should.

Of course it does. It's a mirror.

But I swear when I threw the shards away, my reflection flipped me off.

2. "OTHER" BRANDON

"BRANDON!"

Someone pounds on my door, hard enough that it sounds like it's the third or fourth knock, not the first. I jerk my head up and wince as my face pries itself from the keyboard. My laptop screen flashes to life. I squint as it comes into focus, cursor blinking after the random set of characters my cheek pushed, underneath a message that says RUN SUCCESSFUL.

Above that, it says ZOOMFISH.

What the—

"Brandon! Don't you have class at seven-thirty?"

I check the clock. Eight-twenty A.M., meaning I've already missed first period and will be running on three hours' sleep. Last I looked, it was five A.M. and I still hadn't found the damn virus. The activity log on my laptop claims I didn't even turn my computer on until nine last night, an hour after my new stalker made his threats.

Like it never happened.

"I'll take this thing off by its hinges," Dad says, rattling the handle. "What did you do to this lock?"

I breathe out and slog across the room, push a key code into the box by the door, and twist open the knob. Dad glares up at me (he has to glare up at *everyone*, even Mom) and adjusts his nerd's glasses. I'd say he looks mad, but he always looks like that.

"God, you're a waste of talent," he says. "You can build code locks but you can't do better than a C in history?"

"Missed you, too," I grumble.

"Save it. I'm supposed to be on a conference call with London right now, after getting absolutely no sleep on the redeye from Atlanta. But no, instead I'm excusing myself to see if my *high school junior* has got himself to class yet. Did you sleep in all last week while I was gone?"

I think about that and make a face. Not because I ditched, but because . . . I didn't. Because I started meeting Emma before school—

"Brandon, when are you going to grow up?" Dad shouts. "I shouldn't have to babysit you at seventeen! Dammit, I—" His face pinches. A muscle works in his jaw as he pokes a bony finger into my chest. "Get your things. You have ten minutes, then I'm driving you to school."

"What?" I say, though it's more of a squeak (shut up) because I can't decide if I'm stoked he's driving me or terrified to be dropped off in public. "No, I'll get ready fast, I'll drive myself—"

"No. I'm done with your games. What are you missing right now?"

"Creative writing. It's a joke."

"Oh, which means you're getting an A, of course, so you can afford to skip?"

I close my mouth.

"Did you do your homework this weekend?"

"Yeah." It's mostly true. Somewhat true. The more Dad gives me that soul-piercing look, the less sure I am. "I mean, some of it—"

"Nine minutes left. After school, I'm picking you up and you're coming right home and sitting in that living room until I say you can leave."

He slams the door in my face.

I'm too shocked that he's going to make London wait—so he can drive *me*—to yell my usual snappy comeback. I trace the knuckle dent in my dresser and pull out a Rage Against the Machine tee. Grab a pair of old school jeans off the floor, then it's combat boots over those, a black leather wristband that makes Dad grind his teeth, just need to make sure my hair's jacked up enough to get the same reaction—except my room has no mirror, so I'll have to use the bathroom's.

I glance at my laptop, lid closed on the desk.

It let me run zoomfish, so everything's fine, right?

I listen for Dad and close myself in the bathroom. Dolphins smile at me from the shower curtain, and I shake my head at the seashell tile and think this room is one of the reasons I never bring anyone over. I guess that's the good thing about moving so often. This theme's a year old, so in another six months we'll have a new house and I'll have a new room I don't show to anyone. And new stuff, meaning a dresser without my fist emblazoned on the front, because Mom is all about "New." Seriously, I've never owned anything for more than two years.

I think of Emma showing me her bracelet.

"It was my grandmother's," she says. She holds her wrist over our unopened textbooks, angel's smile in place. "Grandpa gave it to her, and she gave it to me before she passed away. Now it's like I always have them with me."

I reach for her hand. She doesn't pull back. I hold her wrist and trace the tiny gold chain with my thumb, my pale finger against her tan skin, trying to understand how something this old can still exist. It's like trying to see a new color.

"This helps when you miss them?" I ask.

"Yes," she says. Watching my finger on her wrist. She laughs, quietly. "You're going to think I'm crazy, but I can hear Grandma talking to me sometimes when I look at it. Telling me about the night Grandpa gave it to her."

I turn my arm to see more of my scorpion tattoo. I hear Bev and Eric, my sophomore year friends, cheer as the artist fires up the gun and starts drilling into my skin. I smile.

"Not crazy," I say.

I grit my teeth. I don't want to think about Emma.

And nothing in this house means anything to me.

I search the medicine cabinet and pop a few caffeine pills. Wet my hand and lean toward the counter-length mirror to run it the wrong way through my hair, and—

My wristband is gone.

I stare at my arm and try to remember if I actually put it on. It's not on the floor or the counter. Of course, it would've been the last thing I grabbed, so maybe I meant to get it when I noticed my broken mirror and came straight to the bathroom instead.

I decide that's what happened. I rake my hair back until it looks like I had a run in with a falcon, which doesn't take much considering I slept on my keyboard, then lean in to check how bloodshot my eyes are. They look clear enough, but last night was a bad night and sometimes I get bored waiting for a bot to finish, but I swear I threw out that rubber cement—

My reflection blinks.

I jerk back. It's not possible, *not possible*, to see yourself blink. I don't feel that tired. I won't until after lunch when the pills run out. I watch myself a moment longer, wanting and not wanting to see it happen again, and when it doesn't I go for the doorknob. My reflection goes for the light switch. I yank the door open just as the room pitches into darkness, bolt into the hall, and slam the door behind me.

I didn't touch the light.

But it's off.

Your own worst enemy.

I'm going crazy. Apeshit bonkers. Viruses stay on computers, they don't turn into magic curses. This is what happens when you break a mirror? Not that that makes sense either, because the superstition is just bad luck, not freaky reflections moving when they shouldn't.

Yeah, it's finally happened. I've officially lost my mind.

"Brandon, time's up!" Dad yells from downstairs.

I chuckle to myself, because, you know, that's what crazy people do, and grab my backpack off the floor, where it's sat untouched all weekend. To prove I've further gone off the deep end, I contemplate the thumb drive on my desk awhile, the one that should be full of zoomfish's spoils if it worked like it said it did: two hundred names, addresses, routing numbers and passwords for Bank Pueblo's richest clients. If I leave it here, Bank Pueblo may never find out they've been hacked and the owners of those bank accounts will continue on with their happy little lives like there's nothing at all that can hurt them.

I think of Dad calling me a waste of talent.

I snatch the thumb drive off the desk and flip it into my pocket.

"It's time to straighten up, son," Dad says, as he backs my ten-year-old Corolla out of the driveway. I gaze longingly at the silver BMW Z4 in the garage, which used to be mine before I got three speeding tickets and Dad got sick of shelling out bribe money to keep my license active. Still, it was worth the sacrifice. Dad drove me to school for a whole week after.

"Your mother's working eighty-hour weeks, you know, with not a day off in between. She deserves to come home to a quiet house. You need to think of how hard this is on her, with all the traveling I have to do right now. Yet she still finds time to go to the grocery and clean and fill your pocket with lunch money. It would be nice if you showed some appreciation. No more ditching. No more skipping assignments, and I'm serious this time. You're out of this house as soon as you graduate if you don't have a college lined up, you hear?"

"Whatever."

I slump against the seat and watch the Corolla's side mirror. Dad starts in about other privileges I'll lose (iPhone, Internet, my human rights) if I continue doing what I've done the past five years, and I tune him out because I've heard it all before. Instead I think about third period. Spanish III. Where I sit right next to Emma Jennings.

". . . a total embarrassment for someone in my position. Your mother and I don't understand why you can't just . . ."

The reflection in the side mirror rolls its eyes. I sit straight up, look at Dad, look back at the mirror, then down at my hands. I'm clenching the seatbelt, but in the mirror, my hand unscrews the bar piercing I have through the bridge of my nose, removes it, and tosses the silver out the window.

I stare at it until the reflection flashes, and it's me again—I mean, it's always been me, but now it's wide-eyed, white-faced me—and I feel up the ridge of my nose.

No more piercing.

"Do you have a test today?" Dad asks. "Is that why you're so nervous?"

"Er, no," I stammer, refusing now to look at the glass in case something else goes missing. "It's, um, about a girl, kind of. Not exactly excited to—"

"You and Ginger broke it off already? Could've told you that wouldn't last. Girls like that are only trouble, and she knows we have money—"

"God, Dad, Ginger was six months ago! This is . . . someone else. Doesn't matter, don't want to talk about it, *aaaugh!*"

I jerk back against the seat as my reflection throws both nose rings out the window. It didn't hurt, didn't feel like much of anything, but when I grab my nose I find only the holes where they used to be. I *must* be high. That or it's one of those stupid dreams where your alarm goes off and you eat breakfast and go to school, only to realize you're buck naked, and five minutes later the real alarm goes off and you've never been happier to actually get up.

I'm praying that's what it is. I take a deep breath and run a hand through my hair and sink low so I can't see the mirror.

"Brandon, what is—" The sound of crickets fills the car. Dad fumbles with something in his pocket, almost takes the Corolla up a curb, then flips his cell phone to his ear. "Matthew Eriks speaking. Doug! I'm glad you called, did you get my report . . ."

That's how we pull into the school lot. Dad yacking with Doug and me feeling up and down my face. I jack the door open while the Corolla's still rolling and get as far away from it as the narrow sidewalk allows, but I don't lose any more metal, and Dad's turned around before I even have a chance to look back.

By the time I get inside, I've convinced myself I forgot to put those piercings in this morning. I'm hallucinating about the mirrors because I'm running on three hours' sleep. There's no other explanation for it.

(Here's the game, hacker.)

No other explanation.

I have five minutes until the bell rings to dismiss first period, so I shove my backpack into my locker and grab my Spanish homework and a pen. It's the only homework I did this weekend, since Emma and I did it together.

Before she ruined everything.

Before she said—

I grit my teeth and stuff the paper in the trash.

I take my usual route down maroon hallways; right, left, left, and I'm in The Corner, a small area that opens to the second floor. Sometimes kids throw crap off the balcony, but they've known for a while now not to throw anything at me. The sun shifts down from windows in the ceiling. I slide against the wall just outside the light. Press my fingers along my nose until I realize what I'm doing and promptly pull out my phone.

The thumb drive in my pocket burns like a hot coal. I fish it out and plug the adaptor into the phone to check that the accounts are actually there. I don't know if I'm more or less confused to see that they are, but I'm not exactly a stranger to doing things I don't remember, so if zoomfish actually worked, I'll roll with it.

200. You game? I text.

My phone vibrates thirty seconds later. When can we play?

11.5, I type. I slip the phone into my pocket as laughter drifts around the corner, soon followed by the last two people I wanted to see today.

Dad's right about one thing. Girls like Ginger *are* trouble. Candy pink hair, bangs swept over one eye, dark makeup that makes her green eyes promise you anything you want. And always pushing the dress codes, today in a loose black tentacle skirt whose shorter pieces can't be longer than twelve inches, atop torn fishnets and knee-high buckle boots, like something out of a pirate fantasy. Her long-sleeved shirt might've been school legal if the lace in the front didn't dip so low.

I don't need to look at Beretta to know what she's wearing. Kid thinks she's a zombie and bites like one too, and she's always in something dirt-stained and torn.

"Well, well," Ginger says in her babydoll voice. "Look who's back in The Corner. Thought you'd switched crowds on us. I can totally picture you in Calvin Klein."

I shoot her a glare and pull my phone back out. Ginger saunters over, darkening my screen with her shadow.

"Branching out to corrupt the innocent now, are you?" she says. "Or maybe you're going soft on us."

My phone buzzes. I tap to open the message and then Ginger's finger is on my nose, where the metal between my eyes used to be. I grab her hand and squeeze, hard.

"Ouch, Brandon, damn!" She pulls away, then raises an eyebrow. "So if you're not going soft . . . did you do any corrupting while you were gone?"

See you then, says the message from my contact. I think about fifty grand, about the ZR1 Corvette I've been wanting, and it must bring a smile to my face because Ginger squeals.

"No!" she says, hand to her mouth. "You took Emma Jennings's v-card, didn't you? Dog!"

"What?" Beretta shouts, fingers frozen over her smartphone. "And you haven't burst into flames yet?"

"Ginge, shut *up*!" I say. "I didn't take any v-cards. Emma's just been helping me with Spanish and econ, okay? End of story. Leave me alone."

Her smile softens. "Baby, you haven't called me Ginge since we broke up."

For once I'd like a girl to exist who didn't overanalyze

everything. I've never been so grateful to hear the period bell, loud and metallic from the overhead speakers, and I scoop up my book and head for the hall. I've almost escaped when Ginger grabs me by the belt loop and swings in front of me.

"You know, I've missed you a lot," she says, tracing a black fingernail over the R on my shirt.

"She really has," Beretta says behind her, fingers flying over her phone screen. "I'm sick of hearing about it, so if you could just get back together so I could hear about something else please, that would be great."

"Forget it," I say.

Ginger trails her finger down my chest and gives me a twisted little grin. "You remember how good I am at making up?"

"Almost as good as you are at being annoying," I snap, pushing her hand away.

"Oh, come on," she says, hands on her hips. "I made you happy."

"That's debatable."

"I won't pick fights about stupid stuff. Promise. I'll limit my texts to very important announcements only." She steps closer. "Everything else was good, right?"

"We're done, Ginger."

I skirt around her, past giant "Deathrow" Riggs and his Goth group. She follows and grabs my hand. I shake her off.

"Look," I say. "The only way you have a chance of spending time with me is if you know anything about trig. I have an assignment due tomorrow and I haven't paid attention half the semester."

She considers this and tries for my hand again. I shake her off. Again.

"Sure," she says. "I'll stop by tonight."

"I meant during school, you know like—" She disappears in the other direction. "Lunch or something."

I'll probably need a restraining order by the end of the week. I sigh and consider the door of Spanish III, which has never looked so much like it might open into Hell, until I remember I'm Brandon Eriks and I'm not afraid of anything. I'm a machine, all gears and wires. Like the tattoo on my right arm.

Gears and wires and not caring a bit whether Emma's inside already.

Not caring.

Not.

3. FIRST I'M GOING TO FIX YOU

THIRD PERIOD late bell rings. I sit in my assigned place in the first row, sweating, tapping my pen on the desk like a crazy person and watching the clock. Emma's seat, to my right, is empty. Maybe she's sick. Maybe she transferred classes. Maybe she moved to Africa to look after orphans.

The kid behind me, a hawk-faced jock named Jason, kicks my seat. "Stop tapping, freak."

I breathe out and make myself relax. I didn't care what Emma thought yesterday and I don't care now. *She'd* been the nosy one, anyway, who noticed I never turned anything in and offered to help. I didn't need her help, but I agreed because . . . okay, because she's hot. And she never interrupted me. And she talked about dreams in between "*Como se llama*" and snippets of *Don Quixote*. How she wants to teach kids to paint, how she wants to run a marathon.

I think about telling her how I wished I could start school over and pull the grades for MIT.

I think about telling her I how want a family that actually cares.

Freaking Emma.

"*Hola, estudiantes, como están?*" asks Mrs. Barreto, clasping her plump hands as she beams at us from the front of the room.

The class drones, "*Muy bien, Señora Barreto.*"

21

"Homework to the front, please. *Tarea al frente, por favor.*"

She gestures forward. The class shuffles, papers move up the rows, and I turn and grab a stack of homework from Jason, who murmurs, "Nice hair." I give him my best "screw-off" look before turning and handing the stack to Mrs. Barreto.

"Nothing today, Brandon?" she says, frowning as she rifles through the names on the papers. "Where is Ms. Emma this morning?"

"I don't know," I say under my breath, and like the devil's watching, the door swings open and in walks Emma Jennings.

One look at her and you know she's way out of my league. White collared shirt, sleeves rolled to her elbows, buttons open to the scoop of her pink sweater vest. Brand-name jeans tucked into tall gray boots. Brunette curls tossed into a bun. Sweet face, the kind that believes in angels and unicorns and miracles, or did until yesterday, I guess. She swallows, tightens her grip on her tablet computer, and hands Mrs. Barreto her assignment.

"*Lo siento, Señora,*" she says. "I had to stay late for Mrs. Penz."

She doesn't look at me the whole way to her seat. Or when she collapses into her chair and sends a wave of peppermint in my direction that makes me think of her laughing. I lean away, as far to the edge of my seat as I can considering the stupid thing's attached to the floor.

I don't care. I don't care, I don't care, I don't—

A pencil taps my shoulder.

"What'd you do to Emma?" Jason whispers.

I sit forward and thumb through my Facebook account on my iPad. Jason pokes me again when Mrs. Barreto turns her back.

"*What?*" I say.

"How was she?" Jason asks, grinning.

I snap his pencil in half and straighten just before Mrs. Barreto looks our way.

"Oh, I get it now," Jason whispers when she turns again. "You made a move and got rejected. You're not really surprised by that, are you?"

Emma makes a small noise that sounds like a snicker. But she's facing away with her hand clenched in her hair and I can hear the strain in it, and then I remember I don't care and I switch to my note-taking app.

"Okay, *amigos*. *Asociarse, por favor*," Mrs. Barreto says, passing out new sheets of work.

Partner up. I toss the assignments over my shoulder without waiting for Jason to grab them, smirk as I hear them cascade to the floor, and look behind Emma to check my options. I'm in the far row by the door, so I've got a wall to my left. There's a couple kids behind her, but they're already chatting with their default partners. Emma realizes the same time as me that we're screwed. She turns to me slow, eyes down.

Jason blurts, "Emma, want to work with—"

"Yes!" she says. "Dave, can I switch seats with you?"

The heavy boy behind her nods, eyes wide, and scrambles to get his things. Then Emma's smiling and chatting with Jason, and just like that, we move on.

That's fine. This is how it should be.

"Hey," I say to Dave. He stares at me like I'm a grenade with the pin pulled, his tiny brown eyes shifting hectically between the piercings in my ears, the ink down my arms, the gas mask on my shirt.

"Um, h-hi," Dave says, fumbling with a mechanical pencil. I kind of want to talk to him about knives or something to really freak him out, but Mrs. Barreto's watching, so I just scribble my name on the sheet.

"How 'bout we just compare answers after we're done?" I say.

Dave looks down, relieved. "Yeah, o-okay."

It's a *Don Quixote* pop quiz. I try to concentrate on question one (Who is Pedro Alonso?) while listening to Jason compliment Emma on everything from her boots to her brains to how glad he is they finally get to work together. I've started on question two when Jason says, "You going to homecoming?"

My pen smears a blot of ink on the page.

"I . . . well, I don't know," Emma says. "Might be out of town that weekend."

"If you're in town, want to go with me? The guys are getting limos and we're hitting The Bent Fork before."

"Um . . ." She pauses. I can feel her eyes drilling the back of my head. "Sure. I mean, if we'll be here, that is."

Jason kicks my chair, twice. I think about running my pen through his eye, but I clench it and get up instead, and I'm pushing out the door before Mrs. Barreto can raise a finger.

I know what she's doing. She thinks I'll change my mind, that I'll regret what I said, that I'll crack and admit she was right about . . . about us being good together. But she doesn't know who she's messing with, and she can't win a war I've already ended. She thinks she's in my head, but this is temporary. This is just muscle twitches on a corpse.

The classroom door clicks as someone opens it. I edge around the corner and into the bathroom.

And stare, with my pulse on panic mode, at the wall-long mirror over the sinks.

It's a mirror.

It's a freaking sheet of glass.

I take a breath and turn on the first sink. My reflection does the same, looking as stupidly terrified. I move my hand to the left. My reflection copies me. I take a drink. It does too. And then I laugh, though it sounds miserable, because I'm finally so messed up that I'm scared of *myself*, and I fill my hands and splash my face. Let the water run while I turn to the wall and tear a paper towel from the dispenser.

I'm wiping my forehead when the faucet squeaks off.

My pulse spikes to hummingbird intensity. No way, *no way* this is possible. Someone else came in while I was washing. Had to. Or I'm still dreaming.

I don't want to but I lower the paper towel.

And turn.

My reflection isn't across from me. It's by the farthest sink, holding a sheet of paper against the glass. *You're not dreaming.*

The paper towel drops from my hand. I want to say that's exactly what it would say if this *was* a dream, but the sweat prickling my neck feels very real. I look, and look again, at where my reflection's supposed to be. My double smirks and lowers the paper. Scrawls on it with the pen I left by the sink, a pen that's no longer on my side of the glass, but only on his.

LOOKS LIKE I FOUND YOU FIRST.

I choke and brace myself on the counter. My heart's pumping hard enough to lift me off the ground, but as much as I want to move, I can't. There's a virus *in the mirror* and I can't more.

FIRST I'M GOING TO FIX YOU, he writes.

He turns the paper over and adds, THEN LET'S TRADE.

He plucks out one of my lip piercings and washes it down the sink. He goes for the second and I grab my lip, but the ring vanishes under my fingers and I watch it go down, too, down on the other side of the mirror where things aren't reflecting as they should. He goes for the bar on my eyebrow. I pry my hand off the counter and spring for the door. I feel the metal slide free as I burst into the hallway and—

It's gone. Three less piercings than I had a minute ago, like I'm going back in time.

There's a virus in the mirror. A virus. In a sheet of glass. "Fixing" me.

I touch the spikes in my ears, counting seven in each one, and steady my breathing. They're still there. I run the piercing in my tongue along the roof of my mouth.

(Did I take something this morning?)

Caffeine pills. Unless I grabbed the wrong thing. Which is completely possible, because Mom has all sorts of unlabeled junk in our medicine cabinet, and that's when all this started, isn't it? Yes, it is, so it must be the pills. They'll wear off soon. They have to. They *have* to.

I lean against the wall awhile, willing my heart rate to lower, until I imagine that thing coming out of the mirror after me and I get moving. I touch my ears every few seconds and chew my cheek. Nothing else goes missing. Maybe it can only change me in front of a mirror.

And now I'm coming up with rules for nutcases.

"Brandon. On your way back to class?"

I jump and turn to see Mom's nemesis, Principal Myer, with his arms crossed over his pinstripe suit and a knowing, stalker-ish glint in his eye. I haven't spent much time in his office the past few weeks because of Em—er, it doesn't matter—but I'm not in the mood to tick Mom off today with another of his phone calls.

"Yeah," I say, and set my course for Spanish. Principal My-er's footsteps follow me the whole way and soon I'm back in my seat next to Dave, pushing my fingers into my temples and focusing on my questions and not looking anywhere else.

The bell finally announces the end of third period. I slip out before most of the kids have gathered their things and head for The Corner, thinking about trig, thinking about fifty grand, thinking about anything but *that* (because it's just the pills, they'll wear off soon and I'll be fine), when someone jumps on my back and wraps fishnet legs around my waist.

I hope she didn't feel me flinch.

"Ginger. *Off,*" I say, untangling her arms.

She giggles and kisses my neck before dropping down, but her smile fades when she twirls up next to me. "You're pale, babe. And where's your shine?"

"I don't want to talk about it."

"You cleaning up for that preppy?" She scrutinizes my ears.

So I'm not hallucinating that my metal's going AWOL. I don't know if that makes the whole thing better or worse, because if she's seeing what I'm seeing then I'm either taking out the metal myself, and what happens in the mirror is what *I'm* actually doing, or—

I don't want to think about "or."

"Just felt like leaving them out today," I say. "And shut up about that girl."

"Mmm, did I hit a nerve?"

She cups her hand around my arm. I'm tired of shrugging her off so I just let it stay there.

"I kind of . . . like it, actually," Ginger says, gazing up at me. "Wait, you still have the one in your tongue, right?"

I make a face at her, but from her smile, I know she caught a glint of the metal. "Why does that matter?" I ask.

"No reason."

She slides her fingers down my arm. This time I toss her off.

"Brandon, we are Facebook official," she huffs, shoving her phone in my face. "See? Status: In a relationship with Brandon Eriks. Can you at least act like you kind of like me?"

"Believe it or not, I have bigger problems than you today," I say, pushing the phone away. "So no, I can't, and when the hell did you send me a request? I would've ignored it."

I flip my phone out of my pocket.

Ginger laughs. "You're not the only hacker I know, you know."

My fingers freeze mid-Facebook breakup. If *she* sent him after me, if *she's* the reason I'm seeing things—

"Sniper said he only changed your status," she says, biting her lip like it wasn't her idea.

I breathe out slow and scan the room for Bruce "Sniper" Collins, but I'm already relaxing. Sniper isn't near smart enough to write a virus, and I'm eighty percent certain the reason he got into my Facebook account is because I gave him my password for a class assignment. I spot him finally, his arms crossed over his doughboy belly, frowning at me across the room.

"Did one of your deals go bad, babe?" Ginger asks, quietly.

"No," I snarl. "And stop calling me that."

"You are so grumpy today." She snatches my phone and spins away. I grab for it, but she drops it down the lacy front of her shirt, evil grin spread ear to ear. "You need to relax. How about . . . you kiss me and I'll give it back, or you can get it yourself. I don't mind either way."

"I can't be late for history. Give it back."

"Make me."

This. This ridiculousness right here, this is why Ginger and

I will never work. Emma never played games like this. Emma
never—

"Fine," I say, and in one move I pin her wrists behind her
back and press my free hand up her shirt, which is when I realize there's a layer under it that's impossibly tight and rigid
and feels a lot like a corset. A few months ago that would've
been enough to find an unlocked closet and see what other
school rules we could break, but now I feel nothing, nothing
but the bottom of the phone, which I yank free. Ginger blushes
mad red.

And I feel nothing.

"See? This doesn't have to be difficult," she says, breathless.

I flip my phone around so she can watch me change my
status to single.

4. TACO HELL

LUNCH BELL RINGS. Eleven-thirty.

Game time.

I take the long way to the east exit because the short route involves a mirror. I've otherwise decided to ignore my little . . . problem. I don't know how long Mom's drugs will last and I'm not ready to make a fool of myself in front of a counselor, so life goes on.

And I have a deal to make.

I push out the door, blink in the Colorado sun, and check the wall for my contact. Jax waits near the corner of the building, strategically positioned in the blind spot of Ponderosa High's security cameras, a black suit against the bricks. Aviator shades. Hair slicked like Mr. Smith from *The Matrix*. I know he's got a gun on him, but for some reason that makes me feel safer.

"Boss appreciates you, kid," Jax says, and I have to move closer because his voice is never more than a husky whisper. He takes a long draw of his cigarette, then crushes it beneath a Gucci dress shoe. "You get Socials?"

"Next time."

I press the drive into his palm.

"That's too bad," he says. "You worried the Project's gonna snatch you up?"

Coming from Jax, I'm not sure if that's an insult or a joke. I try a smile that Jax halfway returns.

"Yeah, I'm real worried my laptop's going to transport me to Mars," I say. "Just like I'm worried I'll meet Bigfoot on my drive home."

"Never know, kid," Jax says, waggling the zip drive. "You turning down a hundred-K by not bringing me Socials is just as crazy as thinking some Internet ghost is going to zap you outta your chair."

I snicker at that, thinking my mirror problem can top any crazy online hoax he can think up, except Jax isn't the kind of guy you snicker in front of. I turn it into a cough.

"How long 'til your next drop?" he asks, unsmiling.

"I'm staying clean at least a month," I say.

Jax pulls a silver tablet from his coat and plugs the drive in, checking my work. Like I've ever given him less than perfection.

Least he'd never call me a waste of talent.

"All right," Jax says, a minute later. "Check's in the mail."

I wake my phone and tap into my account, smiling at the number when it flashes. Two more taps and I've transferred the funds to my cloaked account, where it can't be "accidentally" withdrawn. Or tracked. Or traced.

"Hey," Jax says, "you ever want to work full time, we'll keep you out of trouble."

I know this. He asks me every time and I've thought about it, a lot. Dropping out of school would piss Dad off to no end. And I could get away from prying teachers, prying friends, prying girls . . .

But I see myself in Jax's glasses, and I don't look like I want to say yes.

"I'll let you know," I say.

I have to walk around to the front entrance to get back in since they lock the side doors during the day. I don't remember much of the walk because I'm thinking about the hundred thousand dollars sunning in my account and what I'll do with it. Dad wouldn't be surprised by another tattoo so that's a no-go. Maybe it's time for something big, like that ZR1. Something that could get me in real trouble if the IRS came sniffing around, asking where I got the dough for it.

Then I think a stunt like that would probably land me in prison.

I might do okay in juvie but if they charge me as an adult—

A group of girls makes a wide arc around me, whispering and tittering. The late bell for fifth period slash A-lunch sounds and the crowds thin as I make my way to The Corner, though I almost go right instead of left out of habit, which would have taken me to the lunchroom.

Where I would normally meet Emma.

I turn left.

Deathrow and his crowd glare at me as I pass, which is what I get for being gone for three weeks, I guess, so I sidle in next to Amber, a rocker chick who could probably beat me up, to see where her group's going to eat.

Amber sneers at me. "I saw your Facebook status. You could come if you weren't dating the devil."

"I'm not—"

"Sweetheart!" sings the devil, and I turn and there she is, Beretta on her arm.

I think about juvie again.

"Taco Bell?" Ginger asks, twirling her keys.

"Fine," I say, because I won't be eating otherwise.

"Yes, I'm starving for dead cow!" Beretta says, drumming her fingers on her lips.

Ginger pushes her away, and not gently. "Not you. Just Brandon." She reaches for my hand. I back away. "We have a lot to catch up on."

"Let her come, Ginge. I don't want to be alone with you."

Beretta grins wide at Ginger, who scowls at her until that smile fades.

"Fine," Beretta says. "I don't want to play third wheel anyway. I'm going to see where Deathrow's going."

"Beretta—" I say.

"C'mon," Ginger says. She takes my arm and tows me toward the hall. I look back over my shoulder, but Beretta just shrugs and flashes her zombie fangs.

"You'll be glad she didn't come," Ginger says as we push out the front doors.

I highly doubt that.

A dusty rest stop on the back roads doesn't look anything like Taco Bell. That's what I get for not paying attention, for slouching way down in the seat with my boots on the dash so I can't see myself in any of the mirrors in Ginger's Celica. I peek up just enough to see the hills around us and the ranches tucked into the grass. And a lone group of pine trees that blocks us from view of the road.

I recognize this place, and everything inside me tightens.

"I actually *am* starving," I say. "I didn't get breakfast."

I sit up, catch a glimpse of the right-hand mirror, and sink down immediately. Ginger unclicks her seat belt and crawls over the console, propping a knee on either side of my hips.

"I told you I'd make it up to you. I keep my promises," she says, pulling off her shirt to reveal a hot pink-and-black corset. One of my old favorites.

I clench my fists and keep my eyes on her face. "What part of 'I need help with trig' didn't you understand?"

She laughs and pushes the lock on my seat belt. It whizzes back against the door.

"I don't take trig until next semester." She presses her lips to mine. I grab her shoulders and hold her away.

"And what part of 'it's over' didn't you understand?"

"Please. Prom Queen Barbie has you all confused. I have to intervene. You belong with us, Brandon." She tilts the lever on my seat. It drops horizontal with a stomach-sinking jerk. "You belong with me."

She kisses me again, cold fingertips wandering my waist-line. I don't want this, I don't want *her*, but she seems to be the only one who cares right now and I . . . I need something to distract me. Because I think I messed up. Because Emma wasn't just—I push her out of my head. Ginger's touch feels like dry ice, sparking fire up my veins. I open my mouth to hers. Draw my fingers up her arms. And then something else takes over, something that moves my hands to her waist, then under the sides of her corset, skin on skin, creeping higher, greedy greedy greedy.

Ginger sighs and unclasps my belt. I find the zipper at the back of her shirt. Tug it down. Neon yellow skulls grin at me from her bra, and Ginger moves her lips to my neck, under my chin, then she concentrates a moment on the top button of my jeans.

Behind her, the rearview mirror squeaks.

And that greed flushes right out of my system.

My double's sitting in the driver's seat on the other side of the mirror, adjusting the glass with one hand. It puts a finger to its lips.

Shhh.

This can't be happening. Mom's freak drugs should've worn off by now and even if they haven't, how could it . . . how could it move the mirror? And where is Ginger? I can't see the passenger seat from this angle. Maybe in "other world," Ginger has a double, too, who actually knows something about math and has a Taco Bell burrito ready to go. Other Brandon smirks at me. The real Ginger's hands dip south, making me jump.

"Ginge, your hands are freaking *ice.*"

I twist upright and grab her wrists, eyes on the mirror.

"Then warm them up for me," Ginger coos. She traces arctic fingers up the back of my shirt, but that's not why I shiver.

The mirror turns again.

The top bar on my left ear slides free. Ginger's teeth nibble my other lobe.

"Dammit, Ginger, stop a second."

She sits back. "You didn't already . . . ?"

"What?" I blink, insulted. "No. Turn. What do you see in the mirror?"

She doesn't look. "Someone who's going to be very happy three minutes from now."

"Three minutes?" I want to defend myself, but I just shake my head. "Ugh, that's not the point. *Look.*"

Ginger rolls her eyes and turns. Over her shoulder I see, and feel, my double pluck another spike from my ear. She had to have seen that. The double goes for a third spike.

Ginger studies my face.

"Okay, I think this game would be a lot more fun if I knew what I'm supposed to be looking for," she says. "Do I have something in my teeth?"

She turns again. Another spike, poof.

"How are you not seeing that?" I say.

"Seeing what?" She scrutinizes my eyes. "Are you high or something?"

"Look at my ears. Notice anything different?"

"Mmm, did I pull those out?" Her fingers brush the tip of my ear, over the holes for four missing spikes.

"No!" I point at the mirror. "He did!"

Ginger looks behind her again, then behind me, then feels my forehead.

"Sweetie, I think maybe you're running a fever—"

"Do I feel hot to you?"

She smirks. "Well, not your head."

"Ginger. Please. You don't see it . . . me . . . sitting in the driver's seat?"

She purses her lips and glances at the empty seat next to her. "It's kinda cramped over there with the steering wheel and all, but we can move if you want."

Pluck. Pluck. Two more out, meaning I only have one left in that ear. I shake her shoulders, and yeah, I know what it sounds like and I can't believe I'm telling Ginger but I need someone to reassure me—

"No," I say. "Look. On this side of the mirror, you're here, and I'm here, in the passenger seat. On the other side of the mirror, I don't know where you are, because I'm—*it's*—sitting in the driver's seat, jacking my shine!"

She looks at my ear again, then at my hands, locked on her bare waist. She doesn't see it. She *has* to see it. I squeeze her hips.

"I know I sound crazy," I say, "but when I look in the mirror my reflection moves like . . . like that's a window, not a mirror. He wrote . . . in the bathroom at school . . ."—Frack, she'll probably drive me straight to the loony bin after this— "He wrote he was going to 'fix' me. Now any time I'm in a room with a mirror he takes out my metal, and he can do stuff on this side, too, like switch off the water or turn the rearview—"

Ginger puts a finger to my lips. "Okay, I get it, you're still stuck on Barbie." She sighs and fetches her corset.

"You're not listening. Someone hacked my laptop and said this would happen."

"Hacked *you*?"

"Yeah, said I'd be meeting 'my own worst enemy' and I thought it was a code but—"

She laughs, bitterly. "Okay, stop. I can take a hint. You want to move to Emma's crowd and you can't look like one of us anymore. Kinda cute you feel guilty enough to make up a story."

"I'm not making this up!"

"Babe, just stop talking and zip me."

I do, biting my lip the whole time, and the last earring slips from my left ear. The double starts on my right. How could I be doing it to myself if my hands are on Ginger? But that's the thing, isn't it? It hasn't done much more than take out my metal, and that's hardly life-threatening. So I could be doing it, I guess.

It could be worse. I could be hallucinating that my double's trying to kill me, for instance.

I stop with the zipper halfway up. Is that possible? So far it's done nothing to hurt me, at least not physically. But I can feel the metal slipping out like a worm, so technically I could feel anything else the double might do.

Then let's trade, it wrote.

If I'm writing to myself, what the hell do I want to trade?

"Hey, make up your mind," Ginger says, thrumming her fingers on her knee.

I spin her around. "I'm not making this up."

"I believe you believe it's real," she says, frowning.

"I'll prove it to you. Take out this spike." I point to the third bar on my ear. The side mirror flashes. My double reaches for the same one.

"Feel the metal on both sides," I say. She does. "Now take it out."

"All right, Brandon, whatever."

Another slip of pressure, and she holds the spike before my eyes.

"Now what?" she asks.

I'd expected it to disappear. I blink, glimpse the mirror, see no reflection.

"Um . . ." I've got nothing. My stomach twists like it's wringing out poison. Am I doing it? Am I doing all this to myself?

"It's supposed to disappear," I say, feeling like an idiot.

Ginger shakes her head. "Whatever you're on, I want some."

She shoves the earring into my palm and contorts her way back to the driver's seat. I turn the metal over and over and finally put it back in, my heart going like a drum solo. I'm the only one who can see him. Maybe Ginger's right, as scary a thought as that is. But I feel that same spike slip out two minutes later, despite keeping a death grip on the seat belt the whole way to Taco Bell.

Pluck, pluck, pluck. By the time I've devoured two double-decker tacos, all my piercings, including Ginger's favorite, have disappeared.

5. SOMETHING'S DIFFERENT

GINGER WON'T TAKE ME HOME despite my threatening to tell Sniper she wants to see him naked. I even try begging (not proud of that) and complimenting her shoes and her driving skills, but she thinks I'm being sarcastic, which is mostly true, and we end up back in the school lot. I don't have time to hot-wire a car because Principal Myer sees us there and escorts me to class, this time under the guise of asking how my parents are doing. Or trying, at least. I don't really know how they're doing so I can't really answer him.

I try not to look like I'm on speed in speech class, though I can't sit still and kids keep looking at me when they're supposed to be listening to Cherie Lamplight's boring debate. A redheaded kid, I think his name's Bill, eventually whispers, "Hey, didn't you used to have like, your face pierced?"

I snicker, even though that makes Mrs. Evans look up, because seriously?

"*You're* on the honor roll?" I say.

But I keep touching my face, biting my lip where the rings used to be, running my tongue through my teeth. Obviously my subconscious wants to get rid of them, but why? They're some of the only things that are mine. I've had the piercings in my ears the longest, got them as a freshman in Albany, New York, along with George, the only kid I'll ever label a best friend because he was just as messed up. My lips and nose were next, all five in tiny Ayer, Massachusetts, the first half of my sophomore year, with Bev and Eric. Those kids knew how to party. And how to hack. Finally, my eyebrow (on the night I thought I'd bleed to death; don't ever let Ginger near you with a needle) and my tongue (also Ginger's fault, but at least done professionally) here in Parker, Colorado, where I spent the other half of sophomore year and now my junior.

Things with memories.

I think of Emma's bracelet.

Seventh period bell rings. I dodge The Corner on the way out and pace in the grass, watching car after car pick up my classmates, some families smiling, some arguing, some saying nothing at all. But at least they're here.

I wait an hour before phoning Dad to remind him to pick me up.

"Brandon!"

Mom's home. Her yell comes from below in the kitchen, her footsteps now stomping up the stairs. I crank Nirvana's "Smells Like Team Spirit" on my laptop until the surround sound rattles the walls. I *still* can't find that blasted virus. I've checked every new virus database and online threat from the last two months and no one's got a problem like mine.

Which confirms it's just my messed-up head.

(Right?)

My door whacks open. Mom stands in all her fury, strands of hair escaping her bun like Medusa, suspicious eyes darting to every corner of the room. Pencil skirt, heels, ruffled white blouse. iPhone glued to her hand. She shouts something, maybe about the noise. I shrug. She starts for the computer and I click off the audio.

"You just remember those speakers are a privilege. Keep it down when I'm talking to you or I'll rip them right out—" She sees my face. Peers around again like something might drop on her head. "Something's different."

I disguise a laugh as a cough. This moment, right here, pretty much sums up my life. I lean back in my chair and wait.

"Your, um." She circles her hand in front of her face. "You took out all the . . . ?"

"Just for a couple days."

"Oh." She morphs back into war mode. "Brandon, do you know who called me today? In the middle of lunch with the President of Virtua Tech?"

"Your BFF Principal Myer?"

"Ha, ha. *Yes*, Principal Myer called, and I had to excuse myself so I could apologize for my son skipping class yet again, and do you know how awkward that is?" (I almost protest that I didn't skip but then I remember Creative Writing from this morning. It doesn't seem possible this day is *still* not over.) "The President is considering my consultation for a multimillion-dollar engineering project. How do you expect me to convince him I'm the best fit for the job if he finds out I can't even get my own son to school on time?"

"Good question."

Mom opens her mouth and promptly closes it, fists clenched. She glowers at me a full minute before saying, "Yes, well, things are changing. First off, your father is working from home the rest of the week to make sure you're up and out of the house on time. If you don't go straight to school, you'll be taking the bus until further notice. Second, you're to pick up a progress sheet at the attendance office tomorrow."

I shoot upright. "What? One of those loser sheets?"

"Careful, Brandon. Think of what that means since you'll

be carrying one all week. You'll need a signature from each of your teachers that you came to class, on time, and handed in your work. Missed signatures equal detention, where Principal Myer assures me you'll have a few uninterrupted hours to catch up." She grins, eyes sparkling. "We should have done this years ago!"

"But I've *been* handing in my work, for three weeks! This is the first time I've missed!"

Her phone chirps. She taps the screen. "Yes, Principal Myer mentioned that . . ." She reads something, one finger to her lip. "But he's afraid, with your track record, that you're slipping. He just wants you to succeed."

He, not she. I pound the desk and make my laptop jump. "This is so lame! I've been good the last few weeks, I've been—"

"Yeah, okay honey, good night."

She closes the door behind her, still entirely focused on the phone.

Six forty-five A.M. My door squeaks open. I remember I forgot to lock it just as cold air pours from my shoulders to my shins.

"Up!" Dad says, tearing off the sheets. "I've been yelling for fifteen minutes!"

I shake my head and sit, blinking, while Dad balls up my blankets and leaves with them. I had a horrible dream about someone hacking my computer and my reflection moving and taking out all the piercings in my face. And possibly worse, it had ended with the revelation that I'd be toting around a slacker sheet at school. I rub my eyes. Roll my tongue through my mouth.

And freeze. I check my ears, my nose.

No metal.

YOU'RE NOT DREAMING.

I shoot out of bed and rip open the bathroom door.

My reflection stares back at me, pale and untrusting, but mimics every move. I reach for a towel. It follows. But still no metal in my face, and when I check the drawer for my extra spikes, it's empty. Mom must've thrown them away.

It's okay. It's okay, I'm fine, I just went a little crazy yesterday but I won't take any pills today and I'll be fine.

I stall a minute before clicking the door closed and turning on the shower.

I check my back in the glass while the water heats, where three skulls grin at me, one on each shoulder blade and one in the center with a dagger stabbed through it, running drops of inky blood down my spine. Down my right arm is the tat that peels back layers of flesh and muscle, revealing the gears and pistons beneath. Up my left, tiny scorpions crawl from a slit in my wrist, a slit that's covering a scar, each one growing larger as they scurry into a wider gash on my shoulder. I smile. Dad never bellowed as loudly as the day I came home with that first one, and almost achieved orbit when he realized I'd used a fake ID to get it. For an hour I actually had a father who cared what I'd done to myself.

One glorious, earsplitting hour.

Steam curls over the top of the seashell-bordered curtain. With one last glance at the mirror, I step into the water.

Stupid loser progress sheet. I did everything to avoid earning one. Three weeks of good behavior should be plenty for a pass on yesterday's ditching. I squeeze a glob of shampoo into my hand and scrub it through my hair. Now I'll have to linger after class, wait for everyone else to leave, and sneak the form by each teacher before the next class trickles in. So unfair. I'm not even failing! C's and a few B's, thanks to Emma's

involvement. I do fine on most of my tests. I just have no mo-
tivation to—

Dark lather dribbles down my chest. I stop scrubbing. Pull
down my hands. The foam drips from my fingers like tar, coil-
ing around the drain in ribbons. Like ink.

Like hair dye.

I watch it and wish I could be anywhere but here. The
vapor around me thickens.

How? I snatch the shampoo bottle and twist off the top.
Smells the same as always. I've used it for months without a
problem. I drop it back on the shelf, breathe in, and inch forward into the stream.

Black curtains down my body, shadowing the porcelain floor
of the bathtub. I push my fingers across my head in disbelief,
and slowly the color thins to charcoal, then silver, then clear.
I try to pull together any logical reason the dye would wash
out that doesn't involve that . . . *thing*. Because now Ginger's
theory doesn't work. Even if I subconsciously wanted to, permanent hair dye doesn't just wash out. Bleaching takes at least
half an hour.

Shaking, I turn off the water, reach for the curtain, and slide
it aside.

A haze covers the mirror, but I know exactly what I'll see
even before I wipe a patch clear. I uncover a smear of glass
and see only the wall and the towel rack behind me. I clear
another circle.

Movement by the sink.

The *other* sink.

My double's leaning against the door, fully dressed in my
outfit from the day before, tussling a hand through honey-
brown hair. At least I assume it's my reflection. Without the

piercings, the wristband, the never-seen-a-comb mess of black on his head, he doesn't look much like the sulky, unapproachable loner I've worked so hard to impersonate the past three years. Even worse, if I ignore the tattoos, he looks . . . *normal.*

And that's just going too far.

I hit the glass.

"What do you want?" I say.

My double smiles and draws a finger through the mist on the mirror.

I'M PREPARING YOU.

"Preparing me for *what?*"

His smile twists. New words drip down the glass.

THE TRADE.

"What does that mean?"

He clicks off the light.

Darkness chokes in on me like a fist. There are no windows in our bathroom, so the only light's a pale slit of sun beneath the door, not enough to give shape or meaning to anything around me. To stop from hyperventilating, I convince myself that if he wanted to hurt me, he would've done it already. Besides, all he's done so far is take out a few earrings and move some things around. Hardly dangerous. Fear is for people whose moms dress them for school. I sigh (sounding far less confident than I like) and grope for a towel. Smack my hand on the rack. Find the fabric and wrap it around my waist.

Crinkle.

From the counter?

Crinkle, click. Like eggshells breaking. Like bullet casings hitting cement. Then the sound multiplies like snapping bones, arguing off the bathroom walls, riddling my nerves with salt and I don't care if he hasn't hurt me yet. I lurch forward as pieces of something clink onto the tile by the sink, yank on the door handle, realize it's locked, fight off cardiac arrest twisting it free, and finally spring into the hallway and into my bedroom, slamming the door behind me.

Maybe he *can* hurt me. Maybe it's like that *Silent Hill* game, where perfectly normal places disintegrate into rust and blood-laced metal and drop you in Hell, some place with faceless monsters and huge knives. Or, and I feel lightheaded from the whack of my heart in my ears, was that thing trying to come *through?* The Trade. I hear that capital T now, because I can only think of one thing "other" Brandon could possible want to trade with me.

Not that it makes any sense why someone would want my life, but whatever.

Dad shouts a five-minute warning from downstairs. I take a shaky breath and stagger to the dresser. Pull out a sleeveless white shirt and a pair of camo pants. I grab a leather jacket out of the closet and a black knit cap that I'll wear between classes when the teachers aren't paying attention. Whatever just happened, I have no doubt Obran—Other Brandon— will try again. And there are mirrors, everywhere. One in the hall. Three in the car. A giant one at school across from the gym. And of course in every bathroom. Will Obran try with someone else in the room? He certainly hadn't cared about Ginger.

I stop.

I think what I really need is a mental institution.

Dad yells again. I think about telling him, but that didn't go over well with Ginger (and she believes a lot of stupid crap), and Dad would probably just see it as an opportunity to have me committed. The house would be nice and quiet with me gone, and my parents could go back to pretending they don't have a son. Not that that's much different than any other time, but I'm sure it'd be quieter.

I grab my bag and edge around the corner, pressing against the opposite wall as I pass the closed bathroom, and dart down the stairs. Dad lounges in the office to my right, his back to the staircase, typing away on a black laptop.

Tell him tell him tell him, my brain says.

Would you *believe you?* asks the other half.

That decides it. I'm going to have to deal with this on my own. And I'm going to need a faster car to calm my nerves, aren't I?

Obviously.

"Bye, Dad," I say as I step into the kitchen

No reply, just the *tap tap tap* of the keyboard. I've learned these are the perfect opportunities to ask almost any question and get a "yes" without Dad ever remembering the conversation. In this way, technically I *do* have parental permission for all the ink in my skin. I finger the closest key ring on the hooks by the garage door.

"I'm taking the Z, 'kay?"

A grunt from the office. I flick the keys off and close the door behind me. Punch the garage opener. Sunlight glitters up the BMW's slick sides, over the convertible top that's already lowered, over the black leather begging me to sit. I hop in without opening the door, then twist both side mirrors up and tilt the rearview to the right. Jam the key in the ignition. Two hundred and fifty-five horses thunder to life, vibrating into my bones like a shot of espresso.

I'm feeling better already.

I jerk the shifter into reverse, ease off the clutch, and back the Z down the driveway. The door between the garage and the house flies open.

"BRANDON!"

Metallica's "Master of Puppets" blares into the speakers. I wave at Dad, pop the clutch, and let the Z roar up the street.

Before twenty minutes of first period have passed, the change in my appearance has flashed up in sixty-three Tweets and thirtysome Facebook updates, according to I-won't-bug-you-fifty-times-a-day Ginger.

The Z caused most of the fuss. Despite parking it as far from the front door as possible, two of the popular girls (blonde Rachel and some brunette chick) have already sidled up to me with questions about it and complimented me on the other changes.

And somewhere along the way I must've crossed a mirror, because my cap is missing.

I avoided The Corner before class, so my phone's jumping with new texts from Ginger and Beretta and even Sniper, all demanding to know if the rumors are true (Sniper says he'll never "hack" me again if I let him drive the Z). I ignore them. I have plenty to contend with already, between Ms. Hilton asking me if I'm in the wrong class (who am I, again?) and my classmates whispering about my real hair color.

"Hey, how'd you lighten it so well?" Ashley Winkler whispers, after Ms. Hilton instructs us to start a new three-thousand-word assignment. "I've always wanted to go blonde, but every time I try it just turns orange."

"Do I have a sign on me that says, 'something's different, please come talk to me about it?'" I snap.

That must be the case, because throughout the rest of the morning, dozens of jerks I don't know come up to ask similar questions. Where's my shine? Did I finally realize wristbands are for girls? And of course the most common question: why the change? They get harder and harder to ignore, but I do a pretty good job, and soon their guesses pop up on Twitter. Most of them assume my parents threatened military school if I didn't shape up. Others said I'd had a near-death experience or been arrested. Then Ginger suggested, probably in retaliation for my ignoring her all morning, that all this is to impress Emma Jennings.

I really think I might hurt her.

That spreads faster than a keg at a party and by the end of second period I have fifteen new friend requests on Facebook. I've spent a year and a half avoiding gossip circles and have effectively isolated myself at every school thus far, not a single ripple in the water, and now this. Stupid Internet. Stupid Ob-ran. Freaking Ginger! I send her a text while Mr. Butrez signs my loser sheet.

Unfriending you.

To which she replies, Luv u 2.

I have to pass The Corner to get to Spanish. I delay as long as I can at my locker, then make the trek down the maroon carpets and have barely turned the corner when Ginger's shriek hits me like a sledgehammer from across the room.

"Oh my *gosh*, Brandon Eriks!"

And just like one of those dreams where you're buck na-ked, everyone turns. Deathrow. Amber. Sniper. Nervous groups of freshmen who usually keep their eyes on the floor. No one's ever stared at me this long without looking away (except small children in grocery stores), and I set my eyes on Ginger's bubblegum hair and press toward her. She snaps a picture on her phone and weaves away from me, laughing, staying just out of reach.

"Ginger, sweety, come here," I snarl, grabbing for her arm. She squeals and hides behind Deathrow, who turns to me with arms crossed. I glance up, then make to go around him.

"Leave," he says, three octaves below a normal human's voice.

Deathrow isn't someone you pick a fight with. I force a smile and back away, searching for my backup plan. Across the room, Sniper raises an eyebrow at me, and I wave him over.

"Man, you're a bigger freak than I thought," Sniper says. "You can't still be with Ginger, right? She says you're after Emma."

"Will everyone shut up about her? I'm not after Emma." I breathe in, glower at Ginger (who's peering around Deathrow's massive trench coat), and scratch my neck. "And I'm definitely not after Ginger. You should really ask her out."

Sniper frowns. "I don't know, I get the feeling she doesn't like me."

"Don't be such a wuss. She's just playing hard to get." I wink at Ginger and now, *now* she looks ticked. "Don't worry, by the end of it you won't like her either."

I clap Sniper on the shoulder and start for the hallway, well aware of the whispers and chuckles that follow me. Like they know I've lost control. Like they know I've been hiding something all along. The windowless door to Spanish looms between smug grins, and I hear *poser poser poser* magnified in my ears and I jerk open the door and then—then I accidentally meet Emma's gaze, the first time we've really looked at each other since Sunday, and I can't hear anything anymore. Two seconds of surprise, that's all I get before her eyes narrow. She crosses her arms and dares me to say something. I shift my attention to my desk.

I want to tell her the rumors aren't true but I don't know anymore.

It's only fifty more minutes until fourth period.

And I really need to take a leak.

6. THAT STUFF'S PERMANENT

MY PHONE BUZZES five minutes in. A text. From Ginger.
WHAT DID U SAY TO SNIPER?

I wait until Mrs. Barreto dims the lights and loads a presentation on the giant SMART Board screen before replying.
That the meaner you are to him, the more it means you like him.

Her next text is an illegible collection of special characters.
Only good thing that's happened today.

I settle back in my chair. I should be watching Mrs. Barreto go through the new verbs for the week, but my eyes keep shifting to Emma, who has her head propped on one arm and is typing notes as diligently as ever. Her hair's down in spirals of honey-spun chocolate.

I start thinking dangerous things. Like how today might've been different, how the whole week might've been different, if I'd kissed her instead of telling her to blow off. I wouldn't have run zoomfish, for starters, which means Obran wouldn't exist and I could jet to the bathroom right now without fear of abduction. Or maybe Obran *would* exist, but I could tell her about him and she would actually listen.

Which is exactly why I can't have her. Because after all this, I'm still thinking about me.

Like she can hear me, Emma turns and looks right at me, copper eyes ready for war. This time I don't look away. She examines my face, my hair, the tattoos down my arms, with enough intensity that I can practically feel her hands making the motions, and then I start thinking how *that* would feel, and that's the way wrong direction. I force my gaze back to my iPad and close Notes Plus in favor of Angry Birds.

Except Emma's still in my head:

"You're not even trying."

It's last week after school. School library. I'm dying a slow death by Spanish conjugation.

"It's been two hours," I say. "It's Friday. All the words look the same right now."

"Hablamos looks nothing like hablo. C'mon, we're almost done. It's just one more page."

"You know what your problem is?" I snap the textbook closed. I can tell Emma wants to save the worksheet I've smashed inside it, but she holds back. "You're too serious about this stuff."

"College is three years away. Two for you. It's time to get serious."

"I would feel more serious about it from the top of Flanger's." I shove my pen in my pocket and stack my iPad on my Spanish textbook.

"The stadium?" Emma says. "There's no game tonight. It's closed."

"I know," I say. I scoop up my book and tablet and wait for her to catch on. "You coming?"

"Brandon, if they catch us in there—"

"They don't have cameras on the roof."

"The roof?"

I chuckle at how scandalized she looks. "No one thinks back on their life and says, 'You know, I wish I did more homework.' They think back and say they wished they'd seen the city from the stadium roof." I nudge her textbook toward her backpack with my finger. "So. You coming?"

Emma looks at me like I've completely lost it, then at her book.

*Then her sunshine smile flashes into place and she slams it closed, just
like that, not even bothering to save her worksheet so it'll be wrinkle-
free.*

"*Show me,*" *she says.*

It was supposed to be a study break. Harmless, meaning-
less, anything-but-more-verbs-please break. I blame the stars.
There were a billion of them that night, whispering at Emma
to put her head on my shoulder. Witchcrafting my arm around
her waist.

Frack, even *that* isn't working as a distraction. If I don't go
now I'm going to bust a kidney.

I rock in my chair, agonizing as Mrs. Barreto instructs us
to open the day's reading assignment from the class Web site,
then per usual, hands out paper worksheets for our answers. I
glance at one, toss the rest of the stack over my shoulder to
the satisfying sound of spilling paper and Jason's whiny protest ("Seriously, man?"), and slip out the door.

I refuse to go to the closest bathroom after yesterday. Instead
I make for the gym, where the giant mirror stands separate
from the urinals, and the light switches are in the locked coaches'
office. Foolproof. Not that the locker room isn't without other
threats. I've won and lost more than one fight against certain
punk jocks, but the chances of them being there during the
minute I need is slim. I think.

I pass the glass lobby by the central staircase and the empty
cafeteria. Cross in front of the open gym doors to the tune of
squeaking sneakers and shouts to pass the ball. The locker room
waits behind a solid tan door on my right. I push it open, avoid
a trio of laughing jocks who clearly don't recognize me, and
pause around the corner from the sinks. The fluorescent light
off the tile is comforting, but I don't hear anyone else. Wait—
water's on somewhere in the back, one of the showers.

It's absolutely stupid I have to consider any of this. Twenty-four hours and one freak in the mirror and I'm jumpier than a freshman girl, and for a minute I feel a crazy sort of defiance that if I just don't believe it, everything will undo itself. I'll walk to the urinals like a sane person. No evil twin's going to suck me through a mirror.

Though in this case (and I feel the smirk in my lips), Obran's more like the good twin.

Not funny. I have to pee.

Except I don't walk out all confident because I'm a coward, of course. I creep around the wall and examine the paper towel dispensers across from me. Glance down the side I'm leaning against to check the sinks and the stained countertop. Beyond that stand four maroon stalls, the square opening to the show-ers, and three urinals. Over the sinks, no thicker than a quarter inch from this angle, gleams the glass.

The door behind me, the entrance to the locker room, opens. My heart does a jacked-up flip when I recognize the voices, and I curse under my breath, dart past the faucets without looking to my right, and skid to a stop at the middle urinal.

"Yeah, that's what Ed said."

Bernie Reynolds. Big linebacker with a mop of thick black cornrows and an insatiable need to pound on things smaller than him, which is most of the world. But it's the second voice that has me praying for a miracle.

"Think he'll be back in time for the homecoming game?"

Tanner. Senior, star running back, pride of Ponderosa High. Not a huge guy, maybe a couple inches taller than me, but has like thirty pounds more muscle. He's fast, too: broke the school record for the forty-yard dash with his 4.4 second time. Also has the attention of USC and the University of Florida. He's supposedly a nice kid, but I'm thinking Tanner Jennings might make an exception for punks who toy with his sister.

They've stopped in the locker room, debating what impact their quarterback's absence will have on the next game. I finish my business and lean against the wall, listening, waiting, praying they'll leave before shower guy finishes so I can jet back to class without drawing anyone's attention. They don't leave. The water squeaks off. I consider closing myself in one of the stalls, but that's a level of lameness I'm not willing to dive to yet. I start across the room just as Bernie and Tanner round the corner.

Tanner glances at me, and for a moment I think we'll pass each other without incident. Then Bernie smiles and says, "Nice ink."

And it clicks for Tanner. His eyes narrow and he steps in my way.

"Eriks."

I hate this. I want to shove him out of my face, even if that leaves me bloody, but I've hurt Emma enough this week so I don't. I look at him like I don't know him.

Then I make the mistake of looking at the glass.

Neither Bernie nor Tanner reflect on the other side. Only Obran, who's bent over the middle sink, laughing hysterically. *Impossible impossible impossible* is all I can think, and it's like watching a horror movie, like watching someone go alone into the room with the killer, and you don't want to see but you have to—Obran straightens, wipes his eyes, and scratches absently at his wrist. Picks at the skin around the scorpions with his thumb.

Tanner shoves my shoulder.

"Hey, I'm talking to you," he says.

"Yeah, I know, what do you—*arg!*"

A bear trap snaps around my wrist. At least that's what I'd swear if I didn't know better. My skin feels like it's dissolving, and I tighten my fist and swallow the expletives bubbling in my throat as I jerk my head at the mirror. Obran's peeling back the top layer of skin along my scorpion tattoo, the ink lifting like it's printed on rice paper.

"Dude, it's a simple question. Don't get so pissy," Tanner says, eyeing my fist.

I exhale and try not to look like I'm in the most agony I've ever been in in my life. My left arm shakes. I hold my elbow to stop it. Droplets of blood squeeze under my fingers.

"Sorry, something cut me back there," I say, pressing the words through my teeth. Only five feet separate me from the lockers. I sidestep to get there, but Bernie gets in my way and raises a brow. I glare at Tanner, jaw tight. "Can you repeat the question."

"Are you changing for my sister?" he says. "Yes or no."

"No, I—"

I think I invent an expletive with what comes next. Obran's reached my shoulder and torn the rest away in one sudden rip that I swear takes my arm with it. He marvels at the clean skin, turns his wrist to admire all sides, and goes for his right arm. Nails dig into the back of my hand. The whimper it elicits from me is very unmanly.

"Dude, relax, I'm not going to slam you," Tanner says, backing away. "I might've if you'd said yes. But I don't want you around Emma, so we're done here."

They give me weird looks and circle around.

I leap for the locker room and wheel around the wall, my arms boiling from the bone out, worms of crimson trickling down both shoulders. I collapse onto a wooden bench and sit there, waiting to die from the pain, but eventually it fades and I turn my arms to assess the damage. Both tats have melted to blurs. I pass my thumb along my forearm, wincing, and my skin wipes clean under the blood.

Eight hours and nine hundred dollars, gone before you can blink.

Maybe I've been searching for the wrong thing. I keep thinking viruses, but maybe that's not it at all. I grab a towel, wipe the blood off my arms, and stuff it in the trash before pushing out the door. I pull out my phone. Ask the Internet what it thinks about evil mirror twins, but all it gives me are YouTube videos with really bad acting and pictures of babies screaming at their reflections. No wiki articles on how to get rid of one.

New search term: what to do if you break a mirror. New results, one suggesting I turn counterclockwise three times, break another mirror in the light of the next full moon (while naked), or walk backward an entire day.

Any of these rites can be used, it says, *but typically the resulting curse is self-created.*

I think about that a minute.

Then I think the World Wide Web is full of shit.

7. YES, I NEED IT FOR CLASS

I GRAB A BLACK HOODIE out of my locker on the way back
to class. It's one thing to show up with different hair and missing piercings. Quite another to return from a bathroom break
without two very prominent tattoos. Not that I really care what
anyone thinks, but the friend requests have slowed and I don't
want to give them another reason to shove me back into the
spotlight.

By the end of the day, I have seven signatures on my loser
sheet to turn in. Principal Myer himself picks it up at the lobby
and commends me for conforming. I decide that tomorrow,
I'm going to miss one on purpose.

I get two steps out the door when teeth close around my
still-tender arm. For the biter's sake, I'm glad my sweatshirt
absorbs most of the pinch.

"*Off*, Beretta, geez!" I say.

I have to flick her five times in the forehead before she lets
go. She socks me in the shoulder and dances away.

"Hungry!" she says.

"Eat a freaking Twinkie!"

"But I *like* biting you." She grins. "Plus, Ginger said I should,
because you sicced Sniper on her."

I jog down the first set of cement stairs, staying to the edge
of the sidewalk. The parking lot's busy already, people walking

and driving and milling like an ant pile, but my Z's easy enough to spot on the outskirt. I stop dead. Maybe a little too easy to spot.

"Oof, what?" Beretta says, running into me. "Oh."

Blonde Rachel Love lounges against the hood of my car, chatting with one of her leggy girlfriends. I'd rather let Ginger pierce my tongue than talk to Rachel, ever, anywhere, so I feel for the keys in my pocket and hit the alarm. The BMW screams bloody murder. Rachel shoots up like a cork.

"C'mon, Beretta."

I grab her hand and stalk forward. She grumbles something about being used and how boys are only good as snacks.

"Hi, Brandon," Rachel says, twirling a lock of gold around her finger. She and Ginger are like the Heaven and Hell of dress code violations. It's warm for September, but I don't know if it's warm enough for the short pleated skirt that's showing off her fake-tan legs or cold enough for knee-high Eskimo boots. A breeze comes up and she zips her white Gap sweatshirt, just a bit, not enough to cover the dip in her low-cut tee.

"Stay off my car," I say, and to Beretta, "Get in."

Beretta gives me a look like I've told her the zombie apocalypse has started and hops into the passenger seat. Rachel follows me as I tug open the driver's door, then leans over the windowless side after I close it. I do not, do *not*, look down her low-cut tee. More than once.

"I really like your car," she says. "Will you take me for a ride sometime?"

"Same answer as this morning. No." I fire the engine. Rachel backs off, hands up, and purses ruby-red lips.

"I guarantee I'm better than that little gremlin," she says, glaring at Beretta. "If you're finally switching to high class, you need the right girl, too."

"*Gremlin?*" Beretta shrieks.

"Buckle up," I tell her, and turn back to Rachel. "You know, I heard you're the 'right girl' for a lot of guys. Your current flavor of the week not paying up?"

Her jaw drops. She yells something, but by then I've kicked the Z into first and it growls over her protests as I squeal a U-turn out of the lot. I get a honk from a minivan but soon I'm on the main street, weaving in and out of traffic. Beretta fidgets against the leather and smiles at me.

I didn't exactly think this far out.

"I don't know what just happened, but this is awesome," Beretta says.

"Um. Did you drive in today?"

"No. I'm actually supposed to be staying after for a group assignment, but this is so much better!"

I slow the Z. "Crap. I'll take you back."

"No, really, this is fine!" She sits straight up, clinging to the seat, then relaxes back and pushes her hand through her hair. "I mean, this is cool. Like, what do you usually do now? Are we going to hit a party or something?"

I snicker. "What do you think I do after school?"

"I don't know. That's why I'm asking." She flips her phone out and starts snapping photos of the inside of the car, the hood, the trunk, me wondering what the heck she's doing. "Need to document this," she says.

"Document what?"

"The rebellious human male in his natural habitat. Surprisingly did not fall for slutty female bait, so when hunting your type in the future, I'll be sure to use something more tantalizing."

I make a slightly illegal U-turn and snort. "Like what."

"We're going back?"

"Yeah. You said you had a class assignment."

She crosses her arms. "Ginger said that you said homework is overrated."

"I said it's optional. For me." That's the most I want to talk about that. I make an early left so we have to take the long way around, stalling in case Rachel's still there. "And c'mon, I want to hear what you think's more tantalizing than girls."

"Hmm . . ." She peers around the seats. "Fast cars. Bet I'd get a whole flock of you at once."

I smile because she's got a point. Middle of the zombie apocalypse, shiny Ferrari, I'd bite. And be dead, apparently, if Beretta's the one hunting.

I finally turn the Z back into Ponderosa's lot. Beretta picks at her collar. Today's outfit is undead Catholic schoolgirl.

"Brandon, do you think I'm a . . . a gremlin?"

I'm really the worst person to have this conversation with. But I dragged her into this, so I stop the Z in the drop-off area and try to put a sentence together that isn't sarcastic.

"Of course not," is what I come up with. "Your ears are too small."

Beretta makes a face at me, then jerks open the handle. "Yeah. Okay."

I sigh because it's literally hurting me to think of nice things to say. "Hey, girls like Rachel only say crap like that when they're jealous. Don't worry about it. You think I care what people think?"

Beretta eyes my undyed hair. "Well . . ."

"The correct answer is no. You do what makes you happy, you keep people around who make you happy, and you don't second-guess yourself when some jerk makes a pissy remark. Though a little advice, you might want to lose the zombie teeth. I saw Deathrow checking you out, but I don't think he likes those."

The last part is somewhat of a lie. I have no idea if Deathrow prefers zombie teeth or not, but I'd like to avoid future biting incidents. It works, though. Beretta beams her set of brown-stained dentures at me, flushes, plucks them out, and slips them into her backpack.

"Better?" she asks, flashing me a new smile that's perfectly white and perfectly straight and so startlingly normal that I don't say anything.

She hops out of the car. "I'm going to take that as a yes. Thanks for the ride."

She skips up the stairs. I breathe out and crank Nirvana's "Lithium" as I turn the Z out to the street, and think that's enough Nice Guy karma to last me a month.

Or not.

I've barely closed the garage door when Dad confronts me in the kitchen with a turbo lecture about taking the Z ("No arguing, gotta be quick, conference call from China in ten minutes"). I kind of listen, substituting the nice things Principal Myer said for any sentence Dad says that includes "irresponsible" or "immature." About halfway through, Dad pauses, one hand gripping the granite island counter.

"Did you dye your hair?"

"This is my normal color, Dad."

"Oh. Are you getting over that rebel thing?"

Like it's a cold or the flu.

"No. Just, um, experimenting." I shrug. "Project at school. Testing the impact of social image."

"Oh, well, good for you," Dad says, looking uncomfortable

at having to praise me. "That's why you took the Z? If you need it for class, Brandon, you just needed to say."

It's all I can do not to laugh. I thank Beretta, I thank karma, and I say, "Yes. Yes, I need it for class. And I *did* ask this morning, and you said okay."

Dad paces again, then points an important finger at the ceiling.

"All right, can't argue with that. This week only, though. I'm not driving your Corolla to the office. And if you get pulled over even once—*even once!*—I don't care if it's because you paused at a stop sign, I'm taking the keys. Are we clear?"

"As glass."

"Good." He straightens his tie. "Now, go do your homework or something."

Like that's going to happen. I trudge up the stairs, pull my phone out to text Sniper about playing Call of Duty, and freeze at the top. Seven feet away stands the paneled bathroom door.

It's open.

"Hey, Dad, have you been upstairs today?" I yell.

Twenty full seconds later, "What?"

"I said, have you been upstairs?"

"No. Why?"

Echoes of crinkling glass shiver through my memory, and when my cell beeps I jump so bad I have to catch the railing for balance. Sniper's reply: Can't, out w/Ginge;)

"Lame," I say. Not that I'm doing much better, shaking on the stairs, afraid of my own bathroom. I inch toward the door with my thumb over the emergency call button. If Obran did break the glass, I've got to clean it up before Mom gets home and fillets me. Skip class, get a new tattoo, fine. But for heaven's sake don't make a mess of Mom's perfect house or you'll be sorry.

I swing the door a little farther open with one finger. If I reach around, I can thumb the lights on without entering. I do so, back pressed against the wall like James Bond, iPhone armed. A yellow rectangle pops into the hallway.

It's quiet.

I peek into the room.

No icy splinters on the seashell-inlaid floor. No shards reflecting off the sandy counter.

No broken glass. The mirror's intact, perfect and whole and silent, hiding any evidence that it's actually a demon portal. I don't poke my head in far enough to see my reflection. I snap off the light and close the door like it's an Olympic event.

I click my phone and check the clock. Three-fifteen. Plenty of time to jet into town, grab some new dye and earring spikes, and start fixing the things Obran messed up. I'll wait on the tattoos until I figure out a way to get rid of him. I am *not* doing whatever that was in the locker room again.

I turn the music up on my phone, shut my bedroom door, pull off my sweatshirt—

"ARRRRGGGG!"

Obran smiles at me from a new, full-length mirror standing near my window. My entire room reflects inside it. I lurch for the door, smash shoulder-first into something hard, and bounce back onto the floor. My dresser? I glare at the mirror. Obran shakes his head and waggles a finger. On both sides of the glass, the dresser blocks the exit.

I've got to break the mirror. I search for something to break it with, but it seems Obran's thought of that already. I can't find the knife I keep in my desk, or any of my dusty textbooks, or even my boots. It won't fit out my windows without jacking up the screens. Maybe I can hit it. I study my scabbed knuckles and think that's not the best idea. Obran paces on the other side, but he's not doing anything (why?), and finally I snatch a steel letter opener off my desk and go for the glass.

Like my piercings, the handle vanishes in my fist. Obran clutches it instead, and for a blood-freezing moment I think he's going to stab himself and I don't know what that will mean. He doesn't. He flings it at me. I duck, but the opener doesn't get that far. The glass shatters, sliding to the floor in jagged shingles.

Slowly, I inch around the bed toward the wreckage. My reflection—my *real* reflection—stares at me from a mosaic of silver-blue shards on the carpet, looking scared and pathetic but looking like me. I nudge a few with my toe. No Obran. I pick up one of the larger pieces. Make a face into it. It mimics me perfectly. Has Obran . . . destroyed himself? I doubt it's that easy, but I should check one of the other mirrors—

"Brandon?"

Mom. I heave at the dresser in front of my door. It doesn't budge.

"Brandon, what was that crashing?"

I shove again. It yields no more than an inch. How did stupid Obran move it so quickly? I'll have to take the drawers out.

"Mom, go away," I say.

"I'm not going to go away, I'm—" She tries the door. "What are you doing in there? That Ginger better not be over again. I thought you two broke up!"

"We did, like a year ago! I don't want to talk to you right now."

"You let me in this instant or I'm going to get your father!"

I yank out the bottom drawer, full of jeans (Folded? Did Mom fold them?) and shove it aside. Pull out the next one. Gape at its contents. Boxer shorts and socks, all in neat rows, and none of them mine. Tommy Boy, Calvin Klein, Lacoste.

All plain colors. No AC/DC lightning bolts or skulls. My mismatched camo socks have changed to dull argyles of brown, black, and white.

"Brandon, I'm going to count to three . . ."

"Mom, chill." I rustle through the pairs, trying to find anything that's mine. "Did you take my socks?"

Pause. "Why on earth would I take your socks?"

I jerk another drawer out, one that used to hold my old Goth things from my days dating Ginger: belts with poison symbol buckles, spikey collars, chains, armbands, and my small but loud collection of weird ties. Now expensive watches and cufflinks fill the space, tidy as the other drawers.

Not mine not mine not mine—

"One," Mom counts.

"One sec, geez."

I toss the drawer away and throw my shoulder into the dresser. This time it yields, jogging reluctantly along the carpet and back into place.

"Two."

I pull open the door, out of breath. "Mom, I'm not twelve anymore. Quit with the counting thing."

"Could have fooled me," she says. She strides past me and surveys the drawers, starts to ask about them, then shrieks.

"*You broke your new mirror?* That was two hundred dollars! What is *wrong* with you?"

"Mom, I didn't—"

"I can't believe this! I try to do something nice, I thought you must be upset about something since you broke your last mirror and that pretty girl hasn't been over yet this week—"

"But—"

"So I bought you a new one. Per usual, Brandon, my hard work is repaid with your knack for destroying everything."

"Mom, if you'd just listen—"

She waves me off. "You know what? I'm done. I give up. Fail out of school, tear up your room, lose your license. I just can't . . . no time to deal with this . . ."

She stomps out, smearing angry tears off her cheeks, and slams the door behind her. I lose track of how long I stare at the handle. I thought she gave up long ago, but hearing it . . . hearing it stings on a level I didn't think I had anymore. It makes me think of burning things. It makes me think of lighting my room on fire, stealing the Z and my laptop and my lava lamp, and calling it my official emancipation.

I flip a lighter out of my pocket and thumb it on.

"This is why I don't care," I tell myself. I tell the *weak* part of myself, that keeps trying to come out, that keeps hoping for things I have no business hoping for. I don't need Mom concerning herself with me. Or Dad, or Emma, or Principal Myer. I've made it this far alone. I'll make it farther.

The ache fades.

I watch the flame shiver and flick the lighter shut.

8. THEN LET'S TRADE

SINCE MOM DOESN'T CARE anymore and Dad's still chatting it up with China, I snatch the Z's keys and peel down the street. Like nothing happened.

And, I tell myself firmly, nothing did. Nothing that matters, anyway.

I navigate through The Pinery's overpriced custom homes, out onto the highway where I let the Z open up. I press twenty over the limit, thirty over, then screech onto a side street and circle around in the hills for God knows how long before I somehow end up in Stroh Ranch, which was probably a real ranch ages ago but is now covered in cookie-cutter houses so close you could reach from your window to your neighbor's.

I stop across the street from one very particular cookie cutter, with gray-blue siding and white trim and a black F250 pickup in the drive.

I shouldn't be here.

I don't leave.

On the second floor is a room full of Emma's toy horses and picture books and clay handprints from when she was three that have been in that exact room since she got them, because she's never known anyplace else. Through the first-floor windows, Mrs. Jennings grabs a steaming roast out of the oven and disappears around the corner where the dining room is. Where the whole family will be.

The ache starts again.

I take the long way home.

Wednesday morning, six forty-five A.M. I haven't moved the drawers from the floor or cleaned up the spilled glass by the window. Or done any of my homework like Dad ordered after I got home yesterday and asked when we were going to eat. I did, however, invest three very important hours into Call of Duty on Sniper's personal account, which I hacked just to make sure I still could. Not really eager to try anything on my laptop yet.

Someone knocks.

"You awake?" Dad asks from the other side.

"Yeah, Dad. Getting up."

The contents of my drawers haven't changed overnight. Since Mom said nothing about shopping, I blame Obran and his stupid quest to turn me into Justin Timberlake. I step over the drawers and pull open my closet.

And snarl out a chain of words that would make inmates blush.

Pink, peach, lavender, and ivory hang in a hideous display everywhere I look. I've never seen so many collared shirts in my life. Vineyard Vines. J.Crew. Ralph Lauren. All in freaking pastel. I finger through them, desperate to find anything black or grey or even just blue, and whoop in triumph when I catch a glimpse of dark fabric. I yank it out and fling it to the floor like a spider when I see it's a pair of slacks.

I yell another word Dad shouts I should never say again.

Obran's gone too far. Wristbands? Fine. Dye? Whatever. Tattoos? Well, I'm still pretty pissed about those. But corner me into Calvin Klein . . . . And This. Means. War. I storm into the hallway, ignore Dad asking me what's wrong, and shove open the bathroom door. I stand in the way so it can't close on me and flip on the light.

"Give me back my clothes!" I yell at the mirror.

Obran blinks innocently and tugs at the collar of a nauseating baby blue polo he's wearing over tan slacks, and . . . God, no . . . under an argyle sweater vest. Hair combed. Hair *gelled*. The room gets hot, and I touch my head. Needle-fine hair meets my fingers.

"Brandon, what are you—oh, hey, son, you look good!"

Dad stands at the top of the stairs, smiling like I haven't seen . . . maybe ever. I look down at my polo, slacks, and that freaking sweater vest and a funny cross between a shriek and a laugh comes out of my mouth. I brace myself on the door frame.

"I will find a way to kill you," I growl at my smirking reflection, and I slam the door.

"What's that?" Dad asks.

"Nothing. Last day of the project, enjoy it while you can."

I spend the next ten minutes tearing up my room, trying to find a scrap of dark clothing Obran has overlooked. No such luck. Not so much as a black undershirt or boxers. I rip off the sweater vest, undo the first two buttons on the shirt, and roll the sleeves sloppy to both elbows. Swap the slacks out for a pair of "7 For All Mankind" jeans (whatever the hell those are) and fume out the garage door. I hop into the Z, tear the glass out of the rearview mirror and the side mirrors, and toss them next to the trash cans. The engine churns to a satisfying roar.

It's not going to be a good day.

Suck factor one appears, predictably, in the form of Rachel Love, who's parked her yellow Cobalt at the far edge of the lot in anticipation of my arrival. I wheel the Z to the first row to avoid her. She can't trot across the pavement fast enough in her hooker heels to catch me before I push through the front doors.

Suck factor two: everyone else. Yesterday I got a few double takes, a few raised eyebrows, a few snorts of laughter as people read the rumors on Twitter. Today books drop, jaws drop, kids run into walls, and conversations cease when I pass. The president of student council welcomes me to the school and says a very unpresidential word when she recognizes me.

Suck factor three: Spanish class.

First of all, I'm pretty sure Mrs. Barreto hits on me. She says something in Spanish under her breath when I walk in that I Google and hope I spelled wrong, because the only readable word in the translation is "yum." Then Jason takes two minutes to remind me that if Emma's going to homecoming, she's going with *him*, back off.

Then Emma arrives.

I get out my iPad as fast as possible and pull up a game. Emma stands in the doorway so long that someone else comes in and runs into her. She sits next to me. The bell rings. I'm killing my eighteenth zombie when my phone buzzes.

What's going on?

From Emma.

I almost put my phone away. But I'm in a pissy mood so I type back, Some people have an evil twin, I have a good twin. It's not for you, don't get excited.

Emma scowls when she reads the reply. My phone buzzes again.

TOO BAD EVEN YOUR "GOOD" IS ONLY SURFACE DEEP.

Ouch. I glare at her, and she stuffs her phone in her bag and looks pointedly away.

I spend the rest of the day offending curious classmates, ignoring Twitter, and disabling friend requests on my Facebook account. There's no way I'll let the kids in The Corner see me in my current state, so I take the long routes between classes to avoid it. I crack the mirror in the east wing bathroom to keep Obran out while I do my business. I don't get my loser sheet signed, and I don't report to the front office at the end of the day.

I skip seventh period. Instead I use that time to zip to the mall and scour the stores for new hair dye, three pairs of ripped jeans, ten band shirts without a hint of pastel on them, and a collection of grunge stuff that would make Nirvana proud: flannels and old gas attendant shirts, the world's sickest leather jacket, two pairs of combat boots so I can hide a pair in my locker. I swing back home, testing the volume capacity of the Z's speakers with Bullet for My Valentine's "Your Betrayal," which rattles tools off the wall of the garage when I pull in. Smiling, I kill the engine and hurtle the door, reach into the convertible's backseat to grab my bags and—

"Brandon?"

I start, and every muscle in me stiffens as I face the girl who's resting against the frame of the garage. I didn't notice the gold Camry parked across the street until now.

"What are you doing here, Emma?" I say.

"You left early."

"Yes."

"I need to talk to you."

Unfortunately, I think there's some safety thing on the garage door that'll stop it if I try to close it while she's there. I drop the bags and lean against the Z's trunk.

"So talk."

"All right," she says, and for a minute I think (I hope) she'll turn and leave. Then, "First, I want to say I'm sorry for what I said in class. That wasn't fair. It's not true, either. There's a lot of good in you below the surface."

I—she just—

What?

That's so far off from what I expected that I just stare at her. She's apologizing? To *me?* After what I . . . but she can't, she should be screaming right now, she should be telling me how worthless I am and how I'll never let anyone close and how I'm a waste of air.

I should apologize, too, but my brain won't click back into place.

Emma rubs her arms like she's cold. "Second, I really do want to know what's going on. I know you made it clear you don't care, but the last few days have been really . . . weird. And where are your tattoos?"

Her gaze drops and I tug my sleeves, like it'll make any difference, since I just realized I've been flaunting clean skin all day. I decide she must want something else, some ulterior motive I haven't figured out yet.

"It's really none of your business," I say.

"Isn't it?" She laughs. Not the happy kind. "That makes total sense, you know, considering I didn't share *anything* personal or potentially embarrassing with you over the last few weeks."

I smile. "I disagree. Your talent show story was definitely embarrassing."

"I was being sarcastic."

"Well you're not very good at it, are you?"

"Ugh, you are so *infuriating*! You know what I've decided?"

Here it is. I wanted it, I pushed her until I got it, and I'm actually . . . smiling. I've never seen her angry. I want to see how Emma Jennings fights.

Then I never want to see her again.

"What?" I ask.

"You're a spoiled, attention-starved brat who can't make up his mind about what he wants."

"Typical rejection backlash—"

"Is it? This is completely out of line? Tell me, then, that none of the following is true. You whine about your parents never having time for you, but you don't want anything to do with them, yet you'll happily drive Daddy's BMW to school. You complain no one cares about you, you have no routine, your family feels fake, but when I invite you to dinner with my family, when I confess to you how much *I* care, you completely balk!"

I don't like how Emma Jennings fights. But I'm pretty good at this, too.

"And you can judge?" I say. "You've lived in Candyland all your life, spoon-fed everything you've ever needed. You have friends who'd die for you, a brother who'd kill for you, you have no idea what it's like to be alone! I lose everyone I care about. So yes, I've stopped caring. And in two to six months we'll be gone again and it'll be back to square one. Don't pretend you understand. You don't know crap about me."

Her expression twists. She whips out her phone, scrolls to something, and thrusts the screen in my face.

My Z.

Across the street from her house.

"You've stopped caring?" she says. "Then why were you at my house yesterday?"

I stare at the picture. This was not how it was supposed to go.

I look down and say I don't know.

The phone lowers, slowly. I wait for her to attack, wait to hear she's given up as well and I should hurry and jump off a bridge while someone would still notice. But her eyes are soft when I look back, somehow both determined and desperate and . . . understanding.

She shakes her head. "What are you afraid of, Brandon?"

This is what she does. She's good at prying. Good at asking questions, good at digging for pearls on beaches full of land mines. I don't know why she should care. No one else does, and when I push them to this, they take the hint and get out. I can't get Emma out.

I need to. I said I wouldn't—

I lie to her. "Certainly not you."

"Then tell me to leave."

"What?"

"Tell me this was a horrible idea, that I'm wasting my time, that you'll never feel the same. I'll respect that. I'll leave you alone. But mean it when you tell me."

"I . . ."

It's just one word. *Leave.* And she will, and that'll be the end of my suicidal decision to let Emma Jennings into my life. I don't need her. I don't, I don't, I don't.

I open my mouth, and scowl instead.

Emma waits.

"I can't," I say.

"Can't what?"

She's *looking* at me like no one ever has, like she can see to my core, like if I lie to her again I'll get struck by lightning. I swallow.

"I don't want you to go."

I don't remember telling myself to say that but it's out and that's that. Emma's phone hits the concrete.

"Do you mean that?" she says.

Pause. "Yes."

"You won't change your mind tomorrow?"

"No promises."

But she smiles, in a way that reopens the hole in my chest like a flame through paper and I wonder what the hell I'm doing. I can't have her. I'll hurt her again, I know I will—

She dips for her cell, slides it in her back pocket without even dusting it off, and draws nearer. I brace myself against the Z. She reaches for my arm and draws her finger where the gears used to be, her touch so soft, and the ice I felt with Ginger cracks something violent.

She says, "I meant every word I said. Until you don't want me, I'll be here. If you have to move again, so what? That's why they invented phones. And you'll be eighteen next year and you can decide where you want to live on your own."

She's very close, now. Closer than we've ever stood. Close enough that all I smell is peppermint and that ice cracks more and I almost—

"I have to tell you something," I say.

She releases my hand and blushes.

"Oh my gosh, you're not gay, are you?" she says. "Is that what this is about? I mean, it does explain a lot, I just . . . I'm so embarrassed, I shouldn't be pressuring you—"

"What?! Emma, *stop*. I'm not gay." I grab her hand and lift the mall bags out of the trunk. "Come on. I'll tell you upstairs."

She follows quietly, through the kitchen and past the glass doors to the office, where Dad's gesturing elaborately, two fingers pressed to his earpiece. I lead her up the stairs and drop her hand when we reach my room so I can scan for any surprise mirrors. None. The floor's just as messy as this morning, collared shirts and pleated slacks flung in every direction. Emma takes in the ejected drawers, the spilled glass, the open closet with its Easter-themed outfits with wide eyes.

"Wow, it's like you set off a yuppie grenade in here," she says, picking up a pinstriped J.Crew and admiring it.

"It's bullshit is what it is."

I rip the buttons off my blue polo tearing it off. Emma flushes again but doesn't look away.

"What are you doing?"

"Getting back in *my* clothes."

I snatch a Stone Temple Pilots tee out of one of the bags and pull it on. Strip out of the "7 For All Nerdy Guys" jeans. Stupid Tommy Hilfiger boxers—those will have to wait.

"Brandon, *geez*, what if your dad comes up?"

"What if he does? Door's open," I say, smirking. I rifle through another of the bags and grab a slashed pair of RUDE's. "Unless you'd like me to close it."

"You know, I really think you need help. Five minutes ago you wanted nothing to do with me."

"You said yourself I can't make up my mind. Better roll with it while you can."

I grin at her. She looks away, smiling at how stupid I am.

"Put those on," she says.

"Fine," I say.

I turn away and tug the jeans up. By the time I've turned back she's folded five of the discarded polos.

"These are really nice," she says. "Did your parents buy them?"

"No. That's what I have to tell you about."

I ruffle the gel out of my hair and drop into my desk chair. Emma plucks more clothes off the floor and folds them.

"Emma, don't do that. I'll get them later." And burn them.

"I don't mind," she says, but puts down her current stack and sits on the bed, cross-legged. "So what's this big secret?"

"Um . . ."

I have no idea how to tell her. She'll listen, sure, but getting her to believe me? And there's no way, no way I'm telling her about my slightly illegal job. Or why I was running it that night.

I grab one of my new pairs of combat boots. Peel the sales stickers off. Start lacing one up.

"So on Sunday, after you, er . . . left," I say, "I got pretty ticked at myself and broke my mirror."

I nod at the closet door where it used to hang. Emma raises a brow and glances at the other broken mirror, but says nothing.

"On Monday, my um—my reflection moved. On its own. Like, I was in the bathroom, and it *blinked*. Have you ever seen yourself blink?"

It's a few seconds before she answers. "No."

It's a few seconds of me holding the shoelace over the next hole before I say, "I know I sound crazy."

"No, continue," she says, and that's it. She doesn't go off on a tangent like Mom. She waits.

I keep lacing so I don't have to see her face. "Since then, anytime I'm in front of a mirror, it changes something. Took out my Earl. Washed out my hair dye. Peeled off my ink. Like actually skinned it off."

Emma clears her throat. "Okay, I'm really afraid to ask . . . what's an Earl?"

"I think you're missing the point." I sigh. "An Earl's the

piercing I had here." I pinch the bridge of my nose between my eyes.

"Oh, good, okay continue."

"That's really the only question you have?"

She smiles, and I realize she's humoring me. I hook the last lace, shove my foot in and tighten. Start lacing the second boot.

"It can't talk," I say. "But it writes to me. Says everything it's doing is preparing me for *The Trade*."

"The *Trade*? What does it want to trade?"

"You're actually believing all this?"

Emma frowns. "Are you lying to me?"

"No." Maybe just leaving stuff out. "And that didn't answer my question."

She holds my gaze awhile.

"No, I don't quite believe it," she says. "And I do. I believe you're using it as a metaphor for what's happened the last few days."

"So then you believe I've learned a way to instantly remove tattoos and completely swap out my wardrobe overnight?"

"No, but—"

"There's got to be a way you can see him. I tried to show Ginger, but she couldn't—"

"Ginger?" Emma's eyes narrow. "Your ex?"

"Again, you're missing the point." I put on the second boot, offer her my hand and hope I've moved on quick enough to avoid questions about *that*. "Maybe you'll be able to see Obran."

"Obran? Where are we going?"

"Just follow."

She does, until we reach the bathroom, where she pulls back her hand back. "You know, this is really awkward."

"You don't believe me, so I'm going to prove it to you," I say. "There's a mirror in the bathroom."

I flip on the light.

"Oh. Right." She casts a nervous glance downstairs. "Again, if your dad comes up . . . door's open?"

Always the good girl. I smile. "Not this time."

She stalls, then steps in, watching me. I close the door. Point at the mirror and try to keep my heart rate down.

"Like right now," I say. "I have no reflection. I don't see me at all. Obran's somewhere else. What do you see?"

Emma looks at me and back at the glass.

"I see us."

"No, no. He'll come, he always does. Then you'll see. He won't like my clothes. He won't like my boots. He'll change them."

He has to change them. I'm baited like a bag of weed in a high school hallway. Besides, something will happen. I have no reflection right now, so he has to come back. I think of the crunching glass, of something coming for me, and I shiver and wonder what I'll do if that happens again.

"You haven't been changing for me, right?" Emma says, touching my arm. "I don't care about any of that stuff, you know."

"For the four hundredth time, no. Plus, tats don't just wipe off. Skinning takes months, even by laser. Explain that to me."

"I . . . well, how do I even know they were real?"

"You really think I put on the same giant temporaries every day?"

"Could be those nylon things."

I turn and pull my shirt up so she can see the skulls on my back.

"Is that nylon?" I say over my shoulder.

Silence. I jump when her finger traces the lines, and it sends goose bumps down my spine when she follows the drops of ash-dark blood. She rubs part of it and the goose bumps sink deeper, sink into my nerves when she pulls away, and I remember the first time I saw her, the first time I wanted her and thought that's all I wanted her for—

And the first time I realized it wasn't.

"I didn't know you had this one," Emma whispers.

I tug my shirt down and examine the glass. Still no Obran.

"He's not coming," I say.

"Maybe it's because I'm here?" Emma's palm brushes my jaw and forces me to look at her. "Calm down. You're shaking."

"He has to come," I tell her.

"Brandon."

"He *has* to—"

She kisses me.

And I forget about the mirror.

I play nice at first, because she plays nice very well but the longer she plays it, the more jet fuel pulses through my veins, the more I need her and I feel myself slipping and I don't care. I pull her close. Her body curves against my chest and she sighs, the vibration thrilling in my mouth, then her hands slip around my neck and there's no space between us.

Of course I want more. Her kiss is fireworks and engine fuel and I'm not thinking past that, and she gets bolder, and the jet fuel in my blood roars wild. I slip my hands under her shirt. Slide them up her sides. Sneak my thumbs under the band of her bra where they meet soft, soft skin, and she whispers my name, and that's what drives me over the edge.

I press her up against the door. Kiss her mouth, her jaw, her neck while my hands slip around to the clasp on her bra.

"Brandon," she gasps. She says something else about Dad, but then I'm kissing her again and she doesn't stop me. I flick the clasp on her bra and—er, I flick the clasp and it . . . what the hell kind of clasp is this? Like there's a virgin supermagnet holding it together, but I can't see what I'm doing and I laugh into her neck at the stupidity of it, and she giggles until I drop my hands and yank up on the bottom of her shirt. She grabs my wrists or I would've had that sucker off in two seconds.

"I said, I think I hear your dad," she says by my ear.

"He'll stay in his office," I whisper. I kiss the skin behind her jaw light as I can, my body boiling with the need to be closer. Her turn for goose bumps. I pull lightly on the bottom of her shirt, asking this time.

The office door creaks.

Emma gives me a you-said-he'd-stay death glare.

"Brandon? You home?" Dad calls.

The first stair squeals. Emma flips off the light.

"He won't check if it's dark, will he?" she whispers, her hands like vises on my wrists.

I don't answer because I just remembered we're in a room with a mirror.

Crick. Dad's footsteps draw closer, but I swear I heard something else echo off the bathroom wall. Emma leans her head against my chest. *Creak.* The floor? Dad's socks brush past in the hallway and fall silent.

"Your heart is going like, a million beats a minute," Emma murmurs.

Clink. Like a coin dropping on a counter.

Or glass on tile.

"Do you hear that?" I whisper, not daring to breathe.

Crinkle. Clink.

Ting.

"Hear what?" She lifts her head. "I think your dad's going back downstairs."

Crack. CRACK.

Five more seconds, and I'll turn on the light. Obran can't come now. He can't. He *won't.* He's not real, Emma said so, and I close my eyes and try to believe that.

"Emma, remember when I told you it wanted to trade?" I say.

Five (*smash!*)—

Four (*like ornaments on concrete*)—

"Yes, but you didn't tell me what," Emma says.

Three (*like a steamroller over a car*)—

Two (*dead silence*)—

I whisper, "I think he wants to trade places."

One.

I lurch for the switch.

9. OPPOSITE DAY

WHEN I WAS SIX, I stuck my finger between a plug and a light socket. That's what it feels like when I overreach the switch and hit the mirror.

Except this is so much worse. This is like being plugged in, like channeling lightning through my teeth and my chest and my fingers, and I try to pull back and I try to yell but I can't. Something jerks me, like it's pulling my stomach through my arm, and it gets really cold and then—

Then I can't feel anything at all.

I open my eyes to darkness.

Emma?

I can't move my mouth. I touch my lips, but my nerves tingle like an army of ants, numb. I reach to my side, feeling for anything to get my bearings. My hand gropes air. Light flickers like a TV screen coming on, so bright I have to cover my eyes. I blink until I can put my arm down.

And I'm not really religious but I start praying.

What's around me is and isn't my bathroom. The light doesn't hit it right—everything shines in grayscale, just the edges, like chairs in a movie theater. Silver lines the silhouette of the toilet, the cabinet next to me, the shaggy bath mat. No color. Only hints of texture, as though anything in shadow doesn't exist. And everything's in reverse. The toilet's on my left instead of my right. The faint palm trees on the shower curtain bend east instead of west.

The Trade.

The light comes from the real bathroom on the other side of the mirror, where Emma and I—Emma and *Obran*—are still against the door, listening. I'm watching my life on the biggest YouTube screen in the world.

"Is he there?" Emma asks, her voice echoing like I'm underwater.

Obran releases her and looks around the bathroom like a kid at Disney World. He touches the counter. Feels the grout between the tiles. Pats his clothes and curls his fingers through his hair. He smiles at me, and I stand there, stupid, too shocked to move and thinking this can't be real, thinking I'll wake up any minute in last night's clothes, coming off a bad high but no worse for wear—

"No," Obran says in my voice. "I think you've cured me. Sorry if I freaked you out. I won't mention him again."

Emma looks at the tile he'd touched and puts a hand on his cheek. "I think you might want to see a doctor. Really. You're boiling up."

"Yeah, I think I will." Obran reaches around her for the door. "We should probably get out of here before my dad comes back."

That gets me moving. I jump on the dark counter and slam a fist into glass that feels like plastic cloth. It ripples when I strike it, leaving a spidery void in the picture. Obran lets Emma out and smirks at me.

"Game over, hacker," he whispers.

The light goes out. The door closes. Everything around me vanishes, including the counter I'm sitting on, and then blazing white erupts overhead and this time my eyes don't need time to adjust.

The first thing I notice: my ink's back. Scorpions on my left arm, gears on my right. I study my leather wristband, my faded jeans, my Rage tee. I reach for my ears, my face. Click my tongue against my teeth. All twenty-one piercings in place.

The second thing I notice: there's no door in this room. It's a ten-by-ten cube with absolutely no furnishings and no windows. Steel cages protect two rectangular fluorescents above, whose gleam reflects dull against the cement floors, the cement walls. No light switch, no mirror. I can think of only two places that would have rooms like this.

An asylum.

Or a prison.

I hear Jax ask, *You worried the Project's gonna snatch you up?*

Oh shit.

The one thing I didn't search, the one thing I didn't even think about because it's just an online urban legend—

A woman in a maroon suit appears across from me. Literally, out of thin air. Chin-length hair, raven dark. Egyptian makeup and rich caramel skin. Mid-twenties, maybe older. Nice legs, but looks like she might cut me for saying so. She doesn't fidget, doesn't smile, barely inclines her head to look at me.

"Mr. Eriks. I am Wendy." She sounds like every commercial ever voiced by a woman. "Do you know where you are?"

"Frickin' high on something," I grumble.

"Incorrect. You are in the assimilation cellblock. You have been incarcerated for identity theft, tax evasion, bank fraud, wire fraud, credit card fraud, and conspiracy to commit these, all of which are federal offenses. Do you understand?"

The only thing I can choke out is, "I want my lawyer."

"Your request is denied. You have been found guilty and will serve your sentence of twenty years. Do you understand?"

No. No, absolutely not. The Project isn't real. It's a joke. A stupid hacker *joke*.

Wendy stares at me way longer than normal, waiting. She still hasn't moved from her original position, hands clasped in front of her. I don't even think I've seen her shoulders rise to breathe.

"I detect you don't believe any of this is real," she says. "Your reaction is typical of new assimilates. Disappointing."

"Disappointing?"

"Yes. Disappointing: adjective. Failing to fulfill one's expectations or—"

"I know what it means."

She still hasn't blinked. "Mr. Eriks, inducting an inmate is an immense waste of memory, so I will be blunt. You are now a part of Project Duplicity, a private, worldwide movement to remove dangerous hackers from society and repurpose them. Like a fledgling serial killer, your Internet crimes have escalated over the past year, from petty software cracks to identity theft and resale. It is Duplicity's responsibility to prevent future damage. Our supercomputer, JENA, found you on the network and has been tracking your activities. She created a digital replica of your personality from your information on Facebook, Twitter, and your iPhone, as well as natural observations of your behavior by way of mirrors, the technical details of which are classified. She then made moral adjustments to your replica to ensure that while you serve your sentence, your double performs as an upstanding, contributing part of society. In the real world, JENA is overriding your personality with the one she created, enabling her to separate your mental signature from your body and upload you into this digital prison. It is not a physical place you can be rescued from, and you will serve your sentence of twenty years whether or not you understand or agree with the terms of your incarceration."

Even though I'm pretty sure I don't have a throat anymore, I feel something choke me.

The Project is supposed to be Internet superstition. You know, like when you get those e-mail chain letters and if you don't forward them to twelve million people, your best friend will get cancer, your girlfriend will set your house on fire, and someone will run over your dog. No one in his right mind would actually fear getting pulled out of his body and installed on a disk.

And I don't know why but that makes me snicker.

"Is this amusing?" Wendy asks.

"It's impossible," I say.

"Yet here you are. Now if there's—"

"Don't I at least get a toilet?"

I swear Wendy rolls her eyes.

"You're a *program* now, Mr. Eriks," she says, like this is an easy thing to absorb. "Your current image, what you can see and touch, is entirely self-projected. As a human, you cannot imagine being without a body. In time you may find, like the other hackers, that you do not need it."

I study the ink on my arm. If it's not real, I should be able to—one of the scorpions crawls farther out of the scar on my wrist.

I might consider it a victory if it didn't remind me how royally screwed I am.

"This is how Obran changed me?" I ask.

"Obran?" Her eyes click. That's the only way I can describe it, like an old-fashioned camera, complete with the noise. "You mean your duplicate. Those details are classified. But I can tell you there is a distinctive barrier between your Self in the Project here, and your Self in the real world. Changing one Self from the other location is very carefully monitored."

"No one seemed to be monitoring while Obran changed *me* the past three days," I grumble. "He actually *skinned* me. And what was the point of that, anyway, if JENA was just going to swap us out?"

"JENA allows her creations to play with their future hosts before the exchange. It gives the Overseer a chance to observe the duplicate's behavior and ensure he is responding to JENA's commands appropriately. If Obran seemed cruel, it's because *you* are."

I can't really say anything to that.

"If there are no further questions—"

"Don't I get a trial or something?"

"My debrief is finished. JENA will be in shortly."

Wendy disappears, leaving me with the concrete. Concrete that feels like nothing when I lean against it, not cold or rough or hard, just numb.

I look at the gears and wires on my arm. I remember telling myself I was too good to get caught.

I think twenty years is a long freaking time.

I guess I should have expected this. Haven't I learned that no one takes an interest in you until you do something bad? Now I'm stuck here, wherever this is, while Obran lives my life. While he cleans up my grades and squeaks me into a community college. While he fixes my broken relationships, or tries to, though I doubt he cares if he fails because what does a computer care about? And in twenty years, when I'm a thirty-seven-year-old dinosaur, I'll wake up married to a woman I don't know with kids I don't want and a job I can't quit.

Or.

Or I'll wake up alone, in a one-bedroom apartment with a box of leftover pizza, a hangover, and a phone with only two numbers in the contact list: my psychiatrist and my boss.

I don't know which is worse.

"Didn't you want this?" I ask the walls.

I laugh, laugh until it sounds like a sob, like the pathetic, simpering coward I am. All flash and no guts. And no one can hear me, and no one cares, which is really no different than . . .

Emma's hand on my arm. Emma looking at me like I'm someone she can see, not someone in the way, like I'm someone worth saving.

I think I really have gone soft.

I also think whoever decided to store hackers in a computer is a moron.

10. I AM *NOT* SLOW

CONTRARY TO WENDY'S PROMISE, JENA is not in shortly.

I circle, glaring at the blank walls, hoping they'll collapse to give me something new to look at. None of this is real, right? If I'm really inside a computer, this isn't concrete or brick. Nothing physical to break through. Nothing physical. I poke the walls, I push them. I even figure out how to walk up one after I convince myself there's no gravity, but seeing the lights sideways instead of overhead kind of wigs me out.

I do not panic.

I do not make a desperate promise to The Man Upstairs that I'll never fight with Mom again if He wakes me up.

I go at it with my fists. And my feet. And my shoulder. I don't get so much as an interesting indent to stare at. Can't tire myself out, either. Adrenaline, apparently, is nonexistent here. Neither can I break bones I don't have or work out this supernova boiling up inside me.

"JENA!"

My voice echoes back, metallic. I wait. Nothing. I sink another fist into the wall and imagine it splitting and caving under the force, slitting a rift I can peel like fruit rind and—

The entire wall glows blue.

I pull back my hand. The concrete dulls. I look around, verify no random women have popped up in my cell, and place my palm against the cement-plastic. Think of waking up in twenty years looking like a creepy car salesman who drives a van without windows.

The wall explodes. The whole *room* explodes—ashy shards zing over my head, roar past my ears, plunge through me without tearing a scrap of my T-shirt. I duck like that'll make any difference and freak when a nasty piece sticks in my arm; except it doesn't hurt, and I remember it's not real, and it disappears, and I'm fine.

This shit's really messing with my head.

The pieces freeze in midair. I don't know if I told them to freeze or if they decided to on their own. All I know is that beyond the lumps of cotton debris it's endless black, like there's nothing else here, like I could walk forever and never go anywhere.

I wonder if I broke it.

It can't be that easy.

I pluck a suspended clump out of the air and gloat a little, thinking maybe it *is* that easy when you're Brandon Eriks, when a girl flickers to life outside the freeze-frame explosion.

I think she's a girl, anyway. She's young, no older than eight, and there's nothing weird about her cotton dress except that it's glowing white. It's the copper and gray swirls in her skin that creep me out and her navy-blue hair that floats around her face like she's swimming, glimmering now and then with silver electricity.

But mostly it's her red eyes.

"Took you long enough," she says in a bratty voice. "I am unimpressed. By far, you are the slowest hacker to break out of your cell since the Project opened. It seems I have overestimated you."

Slowest?

"That . . . was a test?" I ask, feeling even slower.

"One you almost failed. All hackers must escape the assimilation block before they are permitted to work on the Project. Some are out before Wendy·has a chance to debrief them. You took five times as long. The only reason I am not transferring you back this second and giving you to the Feds is your exit strategy." She appears next to me, jabs a few pieces of cement, and sends them rolling into space. "This is interesting. Was imagining a door too simple?"

"*You're* JENA?"

She gives me a very sassy look, considering she's a program. "Expecting someone else?"

"No, but—" I scowl. "I am *not* slow. I can hack a MySQL database in under—" Wow, I *am* slow. I shut my mouth and JENA cocks her head.

"Are you really bragging about that, in here?" Her laugh is a compilation of five kids' voices and it crawls under my skin. "You work for me now. Each day you will spend seven to ten hours in the development cloud, fixing defects and writing software for my employers. If you behave yourself, I will plug you into the game room after hours. Otherwise you will return to isolation. You will also go into mandatory shutdown once per day for a period of eight hours, to allow your physical brain to rest. This will coordinate with your double's sleep schedule."

The floating debris disappears, and I'm standing on neon green shag carpet in the middle of a tiny steel room where the light comes from slits in the metal. JENA's now a voice in the ceiling, high and innocent.

"This is your workstation. You have five minutes to begin."

If you fail this time, I will have your double check himself into the police station and swap you back out. You know what happens to pretty little boys at real jails, don't you?"

I don't like the word "pretty" and that's the most I want to think about her last sentence. I stare at the walls, looking for anything that would clue me in to what the hell I'm supposed to do, but all I hear in my head is JENA telling me how slow I am.

I'm this close to losing it.

Focus. I don't need a physical computer because I'm inside one. But I probably need a keyboard or something to interact with the machine. I imagine my desk at home, laptop booted and ready. No change. I imagine a keyboard and screen emerging from the wall. Again, nothing.

I haven't been this tripped out since I got my first tattoo.

I swallow. Set my hand against the wall and run my fingers over the glowing cuts in it. I hate that nothing feels right in here—there's no change in texture, no bump when I go over a slit—but what I can feel reminds me of the mirror I punched after Obran's trade. I think of the cement room and picture the metal peeling back.

The silver scatters away like bats. The walls of the room become pale blue screens, and I get excited about that until I notice there's no start menu, no icons to click on. How am I supposed to start working if I don't know what program to open?

JENA laughs somewhere above me.

"Four minutes," she sings. "And not surprisingly, you're taking too long."

I think about what happens to pretty boys in jail and bite my cheek, though all I feel in my mouth is pressure, not pain. I picture a black window popping up on the screen. Four rectangles darken the walls, identical boxes on each screen, taking up most of the picture. *Help*, I think, and paragraphs of text scroll down the windows in alien green to match the carpet, commands on the left and definitions on the right. Or so I assumed. As I actually read them I see phrases like "don't drop the soap" and "jailbait" before they scroll out of sight.

"Three minutes," JENA says.

I take my hand off the wall. The black windows close.

She's screwing with me.

Of course text commands won't work. I'm *inside* the computer, I should be able to talk directly to it. But I have no idea what I'm doing. I don't—

New windows open in the corner of each wall, displaying the rearview mirror of my Corolla. Obran drops into the driver's seat. Fires up the engine. Pulls out of the driveway and heads south, which will eventually land him at Parker PD. Stupid machine. If she's the computer, I should be able to control her, not the other way around. I grit my teeth.

"JENA, open the program for me. Now."

"Bossy, bossy," comes the reply.

The Obran video remains, but four new windows pop up next to it, each displaying a different game. Bejeweled, Need for Speed, Plants vs. Zombies, Pac-Man 3000. They cycle through other games, too, and other programs: Word, Power-Point, an Internet browser, and one smaller window that flashes, *two minutes.*

I've never spent more than thirty seconds getting a machine to do what I want and it's driving me nuclear. I think of the screens blasting apart and ripping down the center like paper. Of some futuristic plug floating in the darkness behind the walls that I can tear out of its socket, and then *I'd* be the eyes behind the wheel of the Corolla, and jerk the car around—

The screens flutter. The picture distorts. In the Corolla mirror, Obran signals, cuts someone off, and makes a U-turn.

"Enough!" JENA screeches, so loud the screens ripple. "I am not your toy. I am decreasing your security access, and you will remain in quarantine until the need arises for it to change."

I snicker. "I thought I was slow."

"You are. One minute left."

Obran makes another U-turn. I sigh and close my eyes, thinking about how it reacts to my emotions, and how I really don't want to work for her. Maybe that's my problem. Maybe I need to want to work.

JENA starts a thirty-second countdown.

I want to work. I make myself think it, because the alternative is being someone's jail pet, and I'd rather do my twenty in here. I want to work.

I make myself believe it.

JENA's at "Ten, nine . . ." when I open my eyes to a transparent box on the screen, blank except for a slender cursor in the top left. The window on the right displays an in-box of tasks with numbers, file names, and descriptions of each assignment. The first item expands when I look at it. I memorize the file name, then turn back to the transparent window. Code flashes into existence, lines of text and numbers and variables.

I think how she manipulated me into this and I almost lose the screens.

"Good boy," JENA says, appearing with her weird blue hair in the opposite corner. "The Overseer will be pleased."

For now, I think.

For now.

11. THE KID IN THE FEDORA

IT'S RINSE AND REPEAT the next four days. Or at least the next four shifts. I have no way to track time, I only know that once I tire of coding, JENA shuts me down, claiming Obran's energy levels have gone critical. The routine is maddening. No breaks for food or bathroom since I don't need them, and being "shut down" means a dreamless, black stretch of time that does nothing to relax me. I almost wish Mom would stomp through the screens with another Principal Myer lecture.

During one of the shifts I start fantasizing about Emma, which results in immediate blackout when images of her room flicker over my coding windows. But seriously, at this point I'd fantasize about anything—chocolate chip cookies, the rumble of the Z, how it feels to walk or touch things; hell, being hungry or thirsty or sick. Just *being*.

I'm ready for a throw-down when JENA wakes me on day five.

"Shift start," she says in her creepy little girl's voice, as the screens flicker to life around my prison. I glare at the ceiling and wonder how the other hackers could ever choose to go without a body when it can convey such useful messages, like both my middle fingers are doing right now.

"Screw you," I say.

"Not an option. You will start your shift."

She opens my in-box for me, twelve new tasks to build a higher-security checkout process for some big shot online auction site. I close it and darken the screens.

"No. I will *not*."

A pause, then JENA appears, a tiny, glowing monster in the small space.

"Then you understand I have no choice," she says.

The movie screen with Obran returns from the viewpoint of my bedroom mirror. Obran rises from my desk, pretty boy hair all gelled, and heads for the door. The ache to dive through the image and cling to my bedframe and yell for Dad is like thirst. Maybe if I'm fast enough, I can get through before JENA stops me. I bolt for the screen. The picture vanishes when I reach the wall.

"Yes," I say, clenching my fist against the plastic where my bedpost used to be. "I understand."

JENA cocks her head, blue tendrils sizzling with energy. "You do not care?"

"No, you evil little twit. I don't care if they tear my hair out of my head and make me eat it. I won't do this anymore, and nothing you threaten me with will work. I'd rather die."

She's quiet a minute.

"That can be arranged," she says. "Your duplicate can continue without you. In fact, he would prefer you did not come back. No one will miss you."

"Then get it over with."

JENA makes a strange clicking noise without moving her mouth. Her expression doesn't change when she says, "Most inmates experience a morale boost after a visit to the game room. I have restored your security clearance to default levels. I will take you to the game room now."

"Game room? You're not going to kill me?"

"I would enjoy that. However, the Overseer has specified I do not, as it would be a waste of two years' investment tracking you down."

I smile and wonder why I didn't think of that before. Because I'm *slow*, I guess. "Which means you never intended to trade me out and send me to real jail, so all your threats have been lies."

"Do not make the mistake of thinking you are not replaceable."

"I must not be that replaceable, or you'd just do it. Do all hackers start below the normal security level?"

JENA doesn't answer. Instead the floor smooths to white tile and the walls zoom back a hundred feet on all sides, and it's so much space after my tiny cell that I feel naked. I wonder what kinds of games are allowed in a prison full of hackers. Suddenly I don't know if I want to find out, since the last time I didn't think something could hurt me, it ripped my tattoos off.

"This doesn't change anything," I snap. "I'm still not going to work even if you set me loose on Modern Warfare for three hours. I want a friggin' Mountain Dew or—"

A green can appears in my hand. I stare, then pluck the top and crack it open to the satisfying crackle of fizzing soda.

"The game room is the only server that can replicate sensory experiences," JENA says overhead. "You have three hours. Enjoy."

It's cold. The can is *cold*. It's a stupid thing to get excited about, but I do, and when I press the aluminum to my lips it's like the first time I got high. Wet sugared lime hits my tongue and I down the thing in six swallows, crush the can, and relish the pain of its sharp corners as carbonation burns down my throat. I toss aside the crumpled metal and think of another. It appears and I crack the top—

"Oh, honey, any sensory experience you wants and you're downing Mountain Dews?"

I whirl, but there's nothing but the distant walls. It wasn't JENA's voice. It wasn't female. The voice laughs.

"I haven't seen you before. You must be new. Love your avatar."

A kid my age materializes five feet away. Dark brown hair under a black fedora with a white band. Striped shirt, cuffs showing under a dark blazer, first two buttons open to his bare chest. Black striped pants, a perfect reversal of the shirt. Shiny loafers.

A fashion program?

"Avatar?" I ask.

"Oh, *you're* the one JENA's been complaining about." The boy smiles. "Rumor had it they'd caught someone so hot he had to be quarantined his first day. I suppose you haven't had a chance to play around much, let alone create an avatar. But that can't be your real nose, can it?" He reappears inches from my face, and I resist every natural instinct not to deck him. "I mean c'mon, at least admit you shrank it or somethings."

The only time I've ever thought about my nose was the time someone stuck a bar through the top of it.

I don't like how close he is.

"Back off," I say.

The boy's purple eyes flash, but he flickers a few feet away.

"Name's Seb," he says. "Yours?"

"If I wanted to tell you, you'd know it."

"Oh, feisty. I'll pick one for you then, Kathy."

"*Kathy?*"

Seb's mouth twitches. "Has a certain ring to it, doesn't it?"

"Whatever."

If this is the worst of the inmates, I guess I can deal with it. I chug my second Dew and toss the empty can. It dissolves, pixelating into the air before it hits the tile.

I think about him saying I'm the only one who's been quarantined his first day.

I think JENA's been lying to me. A lot.

"So, how long you in here?" Seb asks.

I ignore him and think of that ZR1 I wanted, waiting lonely in its lot while Obran runs around curing cancer and promoting abstinence or whatever the hell he's been "reprogrammed" for. The room flickers; flashes of gold and red and emerald glint around us like a picture hidden behind static. Translucent blue lines sketch a winding road and rolling hills choked with maples and beeches, then everything explodes with color— tree trunks burn black against fiery autumn leaves, the ceiling disappears beneath a sapphire-perfect sky, bristles of grass wave in a summer breeze whose warmth tests every ounce of my self-control to not cackle like a maniac.

Four days of isolation.

I sprint for the door of a gorgeous Corvette as it materializes on the pavement, gleaming showcase black in the fake sunlight. I run my hand over its smooth nose, and after so long without any sense of touch, it's turning me on just to pull the door handle. I slide into the driver's seat and run my hand along the wheel. The smell of leather makes my mouth water. I shut the door, reach for the ignition—

"ARG!"

Seb reclines in the passenger seat. His head hits the ceiling when I yell.

"Get *out!*" I say.

He adjusts his hat. "I can't ride with you?"

"No! How did you . . ." Of course, because it's not real. "Look, I've just worked thirty-two hours straight. I'm not spending my free time with Johnny Dressup."

"Thirty-two hours? Oh gosh." Seb rubs a finger along his lips. "I got my first break after sixteen."

"I'm serious. Get out."

"Or what? Going to beat me into submission?" He glances at my arms. "Honey, you need to work out more for thats."

I glare at him, at his amused expression and his stupid hat and his weird eyes that have changed from purple to burgundy. If avatars work the same as the environment, I should be able to override him and lock him out of the car, like restricting access for a user on a file. I think about it. I think how much I *don't* want him next to me. Seb ripples, like he's passing through shadow and back again. His eyes widen. He presses against the side of the car and flashes in and out of existence, then vanishes. I smirk and crank the key. Shiver as the engine pumps five hundred kilowatts of energy under my seat.

"Wow, that's like sex," Seb says from the speakers. I curse and punch the radio, which does nothing but leave my knuckles throbbing. "You might be good at what you know, sugar," he says, "but you're still a newbie. You don't know how to block what you can't see, do you? You're too visual. Typical guy problem."

"Laugh it up while you can," I snarl. "I'll figure out how to block you eventually."

"But would you really want to?" Seb chuckles. "You see, I've been naughty. Prisoners aren't allowed to interact. Not at work, not in the game room. I've found a way to hide myself from JENA and visit other users during the gaming sessions. As long as I'm back where I'm supposed to be at the end of my session, she never knows."

"And she just overlooks the fact that I'm talking to myself right now?"

"Oh, don't worry about that. I've got you covered. Like replacing a security tape with empty footage during a robbery."

I stop thinking about blocking him. If Seb knows his way around, he could be useful. He could save me hours of research. Maybe I can get out of here before Obran completely goody-goodys my life.

"Do you know how to use the mirrors?" I ask.

Seb snickers. "See, I try to be a gentleman and get to know you first, but you jump right into business. I dunno, I think I'll leave, like you asked."

"What? Don't be ridiculous. We can help each other."

"Ridiculous? This from the guy wearing combat boots over his jeans?" Seb materializes again in the passenger seat, eyes trailing me from knees to forehead in a way that makes my lip curl. "It's a good thing you're pretty, or I wouldn't have stayed this long. I can help you. I don't know if you can help me. That's what I'm here to find out."

I have some choice words to share with him regarding the word "pretty," but I say, "So you don't know how to use the mirrors."

Seb draws a finger along the ceiling. "Maybe I do, maybe I don't."

"You don't, or you wouldn't need someone else's help."

"Clever bunny." Seb smiles. "Okay, yes. I need someone to figure out that part. I can cover you security-wise, keep JENA off your back. Only one of the servers gives us access to the mirrors. I can get you there, but that means you have to work during your game hours." His eyes trail down my shirt. "Of course, ten minutes here or theres won't hurt our progress too much . . ."

"Never," I snap. "If you were the last person on Earth, I wouldn't let you touch me."

"Just wait another week or two, you'll feel different. Plus—" Seb grins, and his avatar shifts like a waterfall: shining blonde spirals replace his fedora, his once-square jaw rounds below slender cheeks, his suit contours into a vivid red dress that's barely holding in—No. Gross. I don't want to think about it.

"I can be whoever you want me to be," the new avatar purrs.

"That is *so wrong*," I say.

Seb chuckles, voice low again when he—um, she—says, "Bet I can change your mind."

I'm not staying in this car another second. I jerk open the door and the 'vette explodes into hundreds of confetti squares, as do the road and the trees and the flickering sky, until it's four blank walls and tile again. And Seb, back to his male avatar, shaking with laughter.

"Oh, we're going to have lots of fun together!" He grins and plucks his hat off the floor, adjusting it at an angle on his brow. His smile fades. "But seriously. Last person on Earth?"

"Correction," I say. "I'd hang myself."

"Ouch."

"Look, if you really can bluff JENA's security, I'm in. That's *all* I'm in for."

"Sure, love. But keep in mind you've got competition. I'm the only one who's hacked the security, and I've made the same offer to everyone else. First come, first served. That's how this works. Soon as someone else figures out the mirrors, I'm riding them home and that's tough cookies for you."

"Unless I figure out how to crack the security, too."

Seb's smile goes crooked.

"You'll have to get past me," he says. "I'm not just a pretty face, you know. I've got a few extra layers of protection up to make sure you mean boys don't stab me in the back. Turns out JENA deletes hackers who get past her security. As in, fries your chip and your double gets to party it up for the rest of your body's life. My last partner figured that one out." He pushes the rim of his fedora. "Sometimes I miss him."

Something's very wrong with the way he says that.

"You killed your last partner?" I ask.

Seb shrugs. "I don't deal well with breakups." The gold watch on his wrist beeps. He clicks a button on its side. "Time for me to go, beautiful. See you soons."

He winks and disappears. I'm not sure if I can trust he's gone yet, so I call up a couple more Dews and pace the floor until the caffeine makes it impossible to focus on anything for more than three seconds. The walls shift with my imagination: the jagged peaks of the Rocky Mountains, the Massachusetts forest my friends and I hid in to shoot paintballs at cars, the New England road with my shiny ZR1 growling and the door propped open.

I wonder if I can figure out the mirrors before one of the others.

I wonder if I can download what Seb knows about the security from his chip. We're all programs. I just have to find where we're stored.

I'm thinking about that when I slide onto the 'vette's leather and pass my hands down the steering wheel. I think how Seb said I can't block what I can't see, and I glare at the roof until it shimmers, until it goes transparent as ice. The leather seat's cool against my palms, though it looks like I'm levitating. The 'vette's horses rumble under me but all I see below is the road. I knock my hand against the invisible steering wheel. Grope for the shifter. My feet find the pedals and the engine roars in victory, and I'm in a freaking invisible car.

"Too visual," I grumble.

I shove the gearshift into first.

12. JEKYLL AND HYDE

THE NEXT TIME JENA shuts me down, I dream.

"Brandon? Are you awake?"

Emma snaps her fingers in my face, and I blink at her, blink at the bright lights of Spanish class, and look down at my iPad. Pop quiz for something I don't remember reading. I've typed in the answer to number five as "*tres gatos ciegos.*" Three blind cats. I think.

What the hell?

"Is that the answer?" Emma asks, like she's asked me a hundred times.

"Sure," I say. I scroll to question six.

"Have you been to see a doctor?"

I look up and forget what she asked me. She looks good. Hair all curled and her eyes like liquid gold. We're desk to desk, and I reach over and take her hand. It's soft under my thumb. I can't usually feel things in dreams, but when I wake I know I'll remember that.

"I miss you, Emma," I say.

She gives me a weird look. "You need to schedule an appointment."

"For what?"

"You're not yourself. Seriously."

111

"So I've stopped flipping off teachers and decided to dress like a kid who wants a job." These words come out of my mouth but I didn't tell them to. "Do you normally see a doctor for that?"

"Well, no, but—"

"I'm fine. I'm just tired. I thought you said you don't care about that stuff."

I want to apologize as soon as it's out. I want to hit myself but I can't move. Who knows why you say what you do in dreams? My hands go back to my iPad and start typing the answer to number six.

My hands connected to arms without tattoos.

"Of course I don't," Emma says quietly. "I'm just concerned. You said you've been going to bed at eight all week, how can you be tired?"

I don't say anything even though I want to tell her I haven't been to bed that early since I was that old. My hands answer number six. Move on to number seven.

Emma says something about Jason, something else about tattooing his name across her forehead, but suddenly I'm tired, tired enough to fall asleep, and she asks me if I want to go with her somewhere after school.

I yawn. Again, my mouth speaks words I don't want it to.

"Can't," I say. "I have to—"

"Work tonight, I know." Emma sighs and goes back to her tablet.

And I realize what she just said about Jason.

"Wait, *what*?" I say. "You slept with Jason?"

The kids around us turn and it goes dead quiet. Jason's next to me, looking very interested. Emma shrinks in her chair.

"Brandon, no, I was just proving a point—"

"That's right, Eriks," Jason says, grin split from ear to ear as he addresses our wide-eyed classmates. "Emma's shy about it, but man, you get her in the right mood and you can't pry her off with a—"

I slug him so hard across the jaw that he goes to the floor. Then I'm on him, hitting anything I can, and Mrs. Barreto yells for us to break it up and smacks me with a rolled-up magazine and Jason hits back. The second thing I'll remember about this dream is how much that hurt.

Jason's hours in the gym exceed mine by infinity. Three more moves and missed punches and he's got me in a headlock, and I try an unsuccessful jab of my elbow to his gut before I shove my fingers into his eye sockets—

Someone pries me away. Someone pries Jason off, too, and he glares at me and wipes the back of his hand along his bloody nose.

"Both of you! Principal Myer's office!" Mrs. Barreto barks.

And the last thing I'll remember is the shocked look on Emma's face.

I think of her while I'm working. Emma touching my face, Emma laughing, Emma taking off my shirt—

"Last warning," JENA says overhead, because she's told me three times to focus. I make myself stop because today I can't afford to lose my game time. Seb will be waiting.

Except he's not. After JENA drops me in the game room, I waste a whole half hour bowling, shooting clay pigeons, and drinking beer by a pool before I get antsy and change the walls back to white. Every second wasted is time Obran's left to do what he wants with my life, assuming time works the same way here as it does out there.

I don't want to think about that so I start thinking about the walls. How they're not really there.

I start small, picturing my workstation because that, unfortunately, is where I'm most comfortable. Four walls, two black, two waiting for me to tell them to do something. I mess around with a few commands and get a lot of warning screens that initially give me panic attacks because I think they'll report me to JENA, but I keep going and nothing happens. I get bolder. I ask the computer to give me the names of the servers it's connected to.

It asks for a username. On a pure guess, I put in SEB. I bet he's hacked this stuff before.

He has.

It gives me two server names.

Not that it helps me figure out what they are, since the names are a random mess of characters and letters. I ask it for the name of the game server and it's Z83lf93A or something. But I know one of the servers has to be the cellblock where I work, because that's how JENA gets me here. And the other is . . .

Well, I'm about to find out.

I do everything I can think of to cloak what I'm doing, but this place isn't a normal computer, and at some point I decide to just go for it and hope I'm covering my tracks. I don't try anything fancy. I ask it to open a folder on the mystery server and send me the newest file.

When a movie pops up on the right-hand screen, I think I'm toast. I think JENA's caught me and this is what they play for you before you get fried. The computer asks if I'd like to play all videos tagged with "Target Fifty." I have no idea what that means so of course I say okay.

It doesn't fry me.

It plays a video.

"JENA. Explain," says a woman's voice.

A surveillance video in the real world. A fancy office suite lined with windows on two sides and a desk that takes up half the picture. The woman who spoke looks strict and has just as many worry lines drilled into her face as Mom. Vivien Meng, reads the nameplate on the corner. I tell the computer to pause and zoom in on her title.

Overseer.

I grin like a super villain, zoom out, and tell it to play on.

"I advised Target Fifty was not ready for transplant," says a familiar, bratty voice. I have to squint but I can see her, a tiny JENA projected from a dime-sized implant in Vivien's palm. "Against my counsel you made the switch anyway. This is the result. Hence a leak into the real world after the target consumed caffeine simulants in the gaming room. The personalities are still linked. I am at full processing power trying to complete the severance."

"A *three-minute* leak," Vivien says. "Your primary role is to ensure targets *cannot* leak back into their bodies. Explain."

"I did explain." The hologram flickers. "Links between the duplicate and the target still exist. Not all overrides are active yet in Fifty's brain, and during routine maintenance yesterday, some of the overrides failed, allowing him to wake in the real world. I've corrected the error. Severance is ninety percent complete. Within twenty-four hours it will be at a hundred, and the possibility of a leak will reduce to normal, to less than one percent."

The Overseer closes her hand and presses her fingers into her temples. She reaches for a picture of a little black-haired girl in a white dress, a dress that looks exactly like JENA's, and stares at it until the click of an office door sounds off-screen.

"Marcus," she says. "I thought we were done with these incidents."

The guy who steps on-screen has to be a programmer. A

good one, considering his jeans and his long black dreads in Vivien's spotless office.

"I don't know what you want me to do about it," Marcus says, sinking into a leather couch and making it groan. "We put security and procedures in place for targets that follow the process. We don't have code that handles you overriding JENA's recommendation and making a transfer before the severance completes. You knew the risks."

"I had to make the call. Fifty's double attempted a trade without our permission. You need to lower free will on the replicas."

"This isn't *The Sims*, Viv. You can't just tweak a setting and make things work out. Lowering free will could mean a slew of nasty repercussions—doubles not eating, not sleeping, forgetting which pedal is the brake or the gas. If you want vegetables, hire another lead. I can barely sleep at night as it is."

"We're improving lives," Vivien says quickly. "The changes we make produce happy, helpful vessels that take care of their bodies and the people around them while we remove criminals from the world and put their talents to better use. It's no different than them serving their time in jail."

Marcus mumbles something that sounds like, "Except someone else is living their life."

Vivien goes off camera to the windows. I tell the computer to increase audio.

"No less than they deserve," she says. "They'd make the same decisions as their doubles if they were good people. They'll return to a better life, a fresh start. They'll thank us when this is through." She comes back on screen and leans against the front of her desk. "Just make sure it can't happen again. Unstable personalities will need twice the prep time before they're allowed to interact with their real world host. I want the severance as far along as possible before the introduction is made."

"That'll extend our arrest time," Marcus says, pushing to his feet.

Vivien picks something off her suit. "Three minutes he was awake. Three minutes is plenty of time to have told someone what was going on. Do we have video of the lapse?"

"We can only record what the double sees. If the primary was in charge, the clip will be black."

"Very well. I'll ask JENA to extract the memory."

I check the screen to my right for the date, but that does me no good because I have no idea what today is. I ask the computer about the date and it ignores me.

But it can't be coincidence. These are the newest videos, and I'm the newest target according to Seb.

I woke up. I . . . *leaked* into the real world. While I was dreaming.

I hope that's not the only way to get back to my body because it's hella hard to think right when you're asleep.

"Viv," Marcus says. "Why didn't you report this bug?"

He's pointing to something on a ten-inch holographic screen projecting from his watch. If I needed confirmation, there it is. It's my headshot. With TARGET FIFTY in black under it. Next to it are a ton of readings I can't hope to make sense of, some of them red. Vivien sniffs disapprovingly.

"What bug?" she says.

"Fifty's energy levels have been red for four days. Kid's going to pass out on the street if JENA keeps working him like this." He flips the screen back in his direction and frowns. "Damn, Viv. He's only seventeen."

"And lucky we intercepted him when we did. He's pulling bank accounts, Marcus. Socials aren't far behind."

Marcus murmurs something I can't understand even when I turn the audio all the way up and replay it. He starts for the door.

"What was that?" Vivien asks.

"Nothing. I'm going to check on JENA's fatigue report, give the kid a day to rest."

"Absolutely not. Our control of him depends on keeping his energy low. Besides . . ." She admires her nails. "He produces far better work, faster, than our older hackers. Our clients are very pleased. JENA will follow my orders over yours."

Marcus shrugs. "Your call, of course. But you keep pushing him like that and you're risking another leak. I don't care if he's twice as fast as the rest of them. A person can only work so much before he cracks."

"A person has a body and a conscience. And right now I'm very conscious of the deadlines I need to meet."

Marcus shuffles off-screen. Vivien turns her palm and JENA flashes back up.

"Marcus, one more thing," she says.

"Yes?"

"Do fix JENA's avatar before you go home today."

The screen goes black. The computer tells me, in its voiceless way of new facts just popping up in my head, that it has 520 older videos tagged with my number and asks if I want to play another. I close everything out until the white glow of the game room is the only thing there.

I didn't think anyone could care less about me than my mother. Vivien Meng just hit that one out of the park. I'm a gear in a machine, a means to an end, an animal that has to be controlled. I pull the server windows up and think if that's how she wants to play, fine. I have a conscience. It's the cowardly part of me, the part that hesitates every time I dial Jax's number—

JENA's voice pierces my head so loud the screens pixelate.

"That is enough, Target Fifty. Game time is over."

JENA's in a foul mood with me the next few work sessions. She lowers my security clearance, again, so I have to get her permission to finish some of the tasks on my list. The game room is an insult she throws around to remind me where the good programmers get to go. I say nothing, just work until I can't add two plus two and wake up the next session with her in my face again.

I don't dream.

The third time this happens I decide I'm not working anymore. I've had a lot of time to think about what Vivien said, to think about how I let JENA control me, and I'm done. I'm going crazy in here and I don't care if she fries my chip or steers Obran back to Parker P.D. Prison is better than this. *Anything* is better than this.

JENA tells me to begin.

I tell her to do something I'm pretty sure computers can't do.

There's a click and a small sigh, and JENA's new avatar appears in the corner—one whose hair is now a silky curtain of black, whose skin is pure ivory, whose eyes are still vampire red—and cocks her head at me in a very childish way.

"Have we not been over this?" she asks. "You will work, or bad things will happen."

"I'm not your puppet. I know you've been lying to me that I'm slow, and I want breaks and less hours. I'm going to start coding bugs *into* the programs you give me, how about that?"

"All work is tested before it is approved for dispersion to the client."

I snicker. "I can introduce defects that pass your tests just fine, bugs that only surface for a certain user or a certain scenario. You won't find them before the client does."

Silence. Silence for such a stretch of time that I wonder if she turned off. My screens remain blank, waiting, so I pull up a window and start up a game where shapes fall from the top and have to be rotated to fit the shapes at the bottom. One minute of this and the box abruptly closes. JENA's eyes cast the whole room in a red glow.

"My attempts to obtain permission for your termination have been thus far denied," she says, "but the Overseer will soon understand the logic of my request." She emulates a sneer I'm fairly certain I taught her. "However, I have been authorized to use a pain simulant against you in order to stay on schedule. I have installed the necessary software into your cell. You will work your shift, or it will be activated. You will deliver clean code, or you will undergo sessions of it for each deliberate bug found. Do you understand?"

"What if I like pain?"

I'm not trying to be a hero. To feel something, anything, in here would be the best thing I can think of. Even the thought of her chopping off my hand doesn't trigger any sense of fear or anticipation. I have no heart to beat faster. No adrenaline.

Nothing, nothing.

JENA stares.

"Pain, by definition," she says, "is physical, mental, or emotional suffering or torment. The Overseer has authorized the use of all three, but she does not believe physical pain is our best option, in your case. Your double has reported to us your affection for a certain Emma Jennings. This can go one of two ways. Work your shifts properly, and I will ensure your relationship with Emma remains in your favor. Refuse, and I will use your double to hurt her."

I laugh. I'm used to losing people I care about, and this will be no different. I have no weaknesses. I have nothing to lose. Doesn't matter if I behave because one, JENA is a liar; two, it's highly doubtful Emma will stick around long enough for it to matter anyway; and three, I don't care.

I'm Brandon Eriks and I don't freaking care.

"That brunette pinup?" I say. "Do your worst. I can't add her v-card to my stack from here, so as far as I'm concerned, she's trash. In twenty years I'll want something younger."

"Shall I have your double repeat that?"

A video screen materializes on the opposite wall, an Obran's eye view of Emma as they walk through the halls at school, hand in hand. I tell myself I don't feel anything. I can't, not without a heart, not without a conscience. I am a machine.

All gears and wires.

The creature Emma's falling for isn't me, anyway. I *want* JENA to end it. I want JENA to cut her free so she can go her way and find someone who isn't broken, who isn't lying to her, who can make her happy without making her cry.

On screen, Obran stops and turns Emma toward him. I feel something, just a little something, tug at my nonexistent chest.

Emma smiles and that tug pulls more.

"What?" she asks, from a distance that's galaxy-wide.

"Your emotional response," JENA says, "conflicts with your words. Are you ready to work?"

"Screw you," I say.

Except that's what Emma looked like the night I broke her heart. Before I broke it, I mean. Hopeful and happy, trusting me, so sure I felt the same and I—

I know what she'll look like when Obran repeats what I said. The way her face will fall. The way she'll move away from me as fast as possible. Only this time, she won't show up in my garage with an apology she doesn't owe me.

This is it if I let him.

This is how I'll free her.

"Emma, I have to ask you something," Obran says on-screen. "We've been dating a few weeks now, right?"

"Yes," Emma says, looking skeptical.

"There's really only one thing I want from you. I think it's time you paid up. Why haven't you—"

"STOP."

I must have said that last word because JENA's looking at me, a victorious glint in her evil little eyes. My hand is on the screen where the picture has frozen. That tug from before is now a carjack ripping open my chest.

I can't.

I can't let Emma go.

"I'll work," I say. "I'll work, just please don't—" I hate myself. I'm weak and I hate myself. "Please don't turn Emma against me."

"Very well."

Obran says, "Taken me hiking at Cheyenne Canyon?" and the clip disappears.

I swallow, though it feels like nothing, and pull up my task list.

I'm shaking when I start number one.

13. WIRED X505

FORTY HOURS, fifty hours, seventy-five hours later, I lose track. JENA finally drops me in the game room for what she promises will be an eight-hour session, a reward for my conformity. I suspect the real reason is that I blacked out halfway through yesterday's list and could hardly put two words together when she woke me, let alone enough thought to open my coding windows.

The walls open out. I slump down and lay there on the cold tile, my arm over my eyes, and think about how much I hate conforming. And about the lawn at the Wisconsin house we lived in when I was five. How you could see the whole Milky Way on a clear night. How the crickets chirped, how the wind sounded through the bushes around the fence. I feel the breeze come up against my face and the grass soften beneath me. I breathe out and try to remember my life before the shit hit the fan.

"People have been on the moon, Mom," I say in my five-year-old voice. It's one of the only times I remember sitting on Mom's lap.

"Have they?" Mom asks. "Did you learn that today in school?"

"Yup."

"And what do you think? Do you want to visit the moon?"

I think my answer is crashing my toy jet into a plastic dump truck. The orange one.

"Did they offer you the job, honey?" Dad asks, sliding the kitchen door behind him as he joins us in the yard.

"Yes," Mom says.

"You don't sound too happy. Isn't it what you wanted?"

Mom combs my hair down on the side that always sticks up. "It's a lot more travel than I thought."

Dad sits in front of me and rescues a construction worker who's about to get run over.

"I thought that's what you loved about it," he says. "A change of pace, a new company to consult for every couple of years. You've always wanted to get out of Wisconsin."

"And away from my mother," Mom says. They laugh about that, which makes me stop blowing up dump trucks and watch them. Grandma is over all the time, but her surprise visits are the best. She brings candies and bosses Mom around.

"I'll never smother you like that, Brandon," Mom says, kissing my head and setting me onto the grass. "You're right, Matthew. This is the perfect chance for us to start fresh. I'm going to call Dale right now and accept."

She kisses Dad and trots back inside. Dad pulls a brand-new silver airplane, still in its box, from behind his back.

"Whoa!" I shriek, because it's one of those ones from the commercials, the ones that actually fly and you can tell them with your voice to light up and take off and fire missiles—"Dad, cool!"

"Thought you'd like it, son," he says as I rip the box open. "We're going to be flying on a real one like this in a month. Up in the sky. Right next to the moon. How do you like that?"

"A real one?" I say, probably in an octave only dogs can hear, because I'm that amazed that I—Brandon—I'm going to be flying. Next to the moon. "Will it fire missiles?"

"Naw, only the Air Force gets missile planes," he says, helping me *fit the batteries into the toy's controller. "But ours will take us to new places. You want to see new places, don't you, Brandon?"*

I wonder if I can remember that plane well enough to create it.

I lower my arm. Open my eyes.

And deck Seb—whose lips have almost touched mine—full in the cheek. He shrieks and jerks back, but I've got at least five days of frustration saved up and I won't forgive him for ruining my first chance to relax. I jump on him and wrestle him into a headlock, and think again that the other hackers are crazy for giving up their bodies. There's nothing like the feel of him struggling under my arm, the burn of my muscles tightening around his neck.

I'm enjoying the shade of purple he's going when the cheater vanishes and floats away in disembodied laughter, then reappears against the fence on the other side. My Wisconsin house stands at my left, rectangular light ghosting through the windows onto the grass. Stars clutter the ceiling. They look endless, look *real*, and I forget about Seb and stare into them.

"Gosh, JENA must be riding you like a pony," Seb says. "It's been a week since your hot little number came up on my monitor. And you just went from like, the Hulk to that dude from *The Notebook*."

"It'll be that dude from *Silence of the Lambs* if you pull that crap on me again."

"Ooh, I'd like to see that. I kind of have a thing for sociopaths." Seb's avatar flickers, then appears four feet away, just out of striking distance. He shifts into the bodacious blonde from the ZR1 and my fists clench tighter. "Surely you can't hit a girl?"

"Blondes aren't really my thing," I say. "And I think I could make an exception."

Seb smiles and changes again, but not to his fedora-topped Backstreet Boy. The girl's golden tendrils darken to chocolate brown, her face softens, her too-tight dress warps into a plaid snap-up shirt and jeans. I take a sharp breath and back away.

"What about now?" Seb says, in Emma's voice.

"That's not funny. How do you know . . . ?"

"Oh, I've been bored, so I tapped into JENA's memory database and found a sexy little recording she had with your name on it. Don't worry, it's only gone viral inside the prison. I can't access YouTube from here."

"*What?*"

"I know! No Internet is really a bummer. I'm way behind on my blog."

Seb/Emma takes a step closer. I edge away and feel that shaking coming on again.

"Change back," I say.

"Why?"

"You're a freaking sicko, that's why. Change back."

Emma's grin widens. "You really care for her. You do, because if she was someone you fabricated or a one-night stand it wouldn't bother you so much. Do you love her?" She appears right in front of me, peering up with amber eyes that make my chest ache. "Do you love me?"

"You? No. Her . . . it doesn't matter. I have eight hours in here, we should get to work on this mirror thing."

"But I'm having so much fun," Emma says, trailing her fingers up my arm.

Which is way more confusing than I should let it be. I know it's Seb, but seeing her . . . seeing her this close, and having anyone touch me, is like giving steak to a starving man. Seb/Emma smirks at the conflict in my eyes. I don't move away. Not when she drapes her arms around my neck, not when she presses her fake body against mine.

She's warm. She's so warm, and I remember what it was like to kiss her, I remember the curve of her back under my hands.

"It doesn't matter who you are in here, gorgeous," she says. "Male, female, ugly, beautiful. Sometimes I wonder if I'd prefer to stay, but frankly, I hate working. I miss shopping for Pumas and I'm way behind on my Facebook stalking. Plus, I miss things like this . . ."

"Ugh, stop it!" I shove her away and shudder, wiping her touch off my neck and shaking it off my hand like spit. "Don't talk to me like that, don't impersonate Emma, and don't *touch* me! You're right, it doesn't matter who you are in here because in reality you could be anyone else, including a fifty-year-old pedophile!"

Seb gasps. "Kathy! How could you say such a thing?"

The stars dissolve. The lawn melds to black steel. Seb shifts to his normal avatar and adjusts his hat with a glare.

"I am *so not* a fifty-year-old pedophile. I'm eighteen, thank you very much, and I expect an apology."

"I'm not apologizing, you tried to seduce me wearing the skin of someone . . . someone I know!"

The dark metal closes us inside a box no bigger than my usual workspace, and I get really claustrophobic. Just like my first day on the job, the only light comes from slits in the walls, small Z's of neon blue.

"Where are we now?" I ask, pulling my arms tight.

"The control server for the mirrors. And now you know as much as I do."

"JENA won't find us?"

Seb laughs. "Won't find me. Won't find you, if you say you're sorry."

"I'm *not* apologizing."

"Five."

"Seriously? You sound like my mom, why would I have to—"

"Four."

"You started it, if you'd kept your hands to yourself—"

"Three."

"There's going to be an asterisk by this apology—"

"Two."

"All right, I'm sorry!"

Seb grins. "Not so hard, is it? Don't you feel better now?"

I would feel better if I could knock him into next week. I clench my teeth, push two fingers into the closest wall, and picture the darkness peeling back. Nothing happens. Maybe because I'm also picturing Seb's face peeling back. I exhale. I don't think about how close the walls are. I replay what I want to do over and over in my head, but the room starts spinning and the light fades and my hand slips—

Seb catches me, and this time I can't connect my brain to my arm to shove him off. JENA must be shutting me down. I fight against it, and instead of blacking out I plunge underwater, choke on a mouthful of liquid salt, and struggle against corpse-green waves that churn like molasses. Someone drags me by the collar onto a bank of dirt-swirled sand. I blink into a shapeless sun and glance around the tiny beach, at the single palm tree on the sand bar, and finally at Seb, who looks annoyed.

"That little slut! I know what she's doing," he says. "JENA must think you can crack the mirrors. She's running you low so you don't have the energy to even think about it."

"We're back in the game room?"

"Yeah, my section of it, anyway. Here, doll." An orange can materializes in Seb's hand. He offers it to me. "Drink up."

"Wired x505?" I read from the label. "It says it's equivalent to six and a half Red Bulls."

"Exciting, isn't it?"

"It has a warning label."

"Honey, it's a simulant. You don't have a body. It can't kill you. And I'm sure you've done worse."

That makes me smile. "Why would you assume that?"

"Oh gosh," Seb says, raising both hands. "I'm shutting my big mouth."

I crack open the top and take three swallows before gagging.

"Ugh, it tastes like someone pissed cough syrup into orange juice."

Seb giggles. "Kathy, JENA did mention you're inside a computer, yes? Digital prison? Your brain is spinning on someone's hard drive? Turn off your taste buds if you don't like it."

I don't have the energy to learn something new so I just grunt and chug the rest. I throw the can at the water when I'm done. It hits the surface and evaporates in thousands of glassy squares.

"How long does it take for this stuff to kick in?" I ask.

"Maybe five minutes? But that's if you had a stomach. I dunno, I've never tried one."

"What? How do you know it'll even work?"

Seb smiles. "Trust me."

"That's the thing. I *don't*. Especially considering what happened to your last partner. For all I know you're using me as a scapegoat in case you get caught somewhere you're not supposed to be. What'd you get arrested for, anyway? Why do you randomly add S's to words? Why are we sitting on a beach?" I stare at the water. "I can turn off my taste buds?"

"Yup, I think it's working. Hold on, love."

The room morphs back to black sheet metal a thousand feet high. The light behind it pulses. I whip my head toward a wall and the darkness peels away, scattering like my eyes are lasers, and transparent screens flash up one after the other. I read about three lines of text before closing one and moving on. I'm on the twelfth screen when Seb says, "Do you have any idea what you're doing? Because I definitely can't read that fast."

I close screen thirteen. It's data, lots of data, on who's used the mirrors and when. How many billions the company's spent buying up glass corporations and infusing nanobots into mirrors everywhere from major construction to cars. How JENA has to conduct the first swap in total darkness since exposure to light corrupts a chemical the bots use to extract the primary personality. But only JENA uses the mirrors, and JENA alone. No details on how. I bring back screen four. One of the most recent swaps.

Mine.

" 'First attempt at a trade with a conscious target,' " Seb reads, his grin widening as he scans the log. " 'Note: JENA advised no-go. Duplicate initiated contact. Overseer Meng approved trade at eighteen hundred. Target romantically distracted. Highly successful, as social protocol prevented target from exiting during preparations.' Stud muffin. Does she mean from the room, or the girl?"

"Shut *up*. Trying to work here."

But there's nothing I can use. The text ends with a few suggestions to minimize the noise the mirrors make while JENA charges them, as the nanobots need a massive amount of electric energy to exchange the duplicate and original personalities.

Says after the initial swap, the light-sensitive chemical in the target's body neutralizes, making future swaps possible in daylight. Meaning I don't have to catch Obran in the dark. But he's got to be close enough to a mirror to—

Seb is *still* laughing.

"What the hell is so funny?" I snap.

"I can't help it. I just keep picturing . . . you finally scoring and getting arrested in the middle . . ."

I don't care enough to correct him. I close out the computer windows and thumb at a shaft of blue light.

JENA responds to thoughts, to pictures I make in my mind. I should be able to picture a room I know has a mirror. Except not the same way I picture the Corvette or Seb's beach or my Wisconsin house. Instead, what JENA sees. Something like the room I arrived in, with its weird reverse furniture and television mirror screen.

Obran used the mirror rooms. JENA may have controlled him, but the log said Obran initiated contact. I should be able to interact with the mirrors the same way he did.

"You were asleep when they took you?" I ask.

"Sweetie, you're talking likes, three hundred miles a minute."

I sigh and tap my fingers on the wall. "You. Were. Asleep. When. They. Took. You?"

"Yeah, and everyone else I've talked to, too. Passed out in front of my computer, woke up in a gray room." He gives me a thoughtful look. "What was it like, swapping real time?"

"Kind of like waking up with you half an inch from my mouth."

"Like the best day of your life?" He cackles, then goes serious. "But you woke up in the gray room, right? Or somewhere elses?"

I almost tell him. Almost, then I shut my mouth and re-mind myself I don't trust him. I have to keep some secrets to myself or I'll lose the only edge I've got.

Because if that's it—

If it is—

That's why JENA's so freaked about my security access. That's why she didn't approve Obran's swap and why she works me until my brain melts, because I saw something she didn't want me to see.

And now I know exactly what I need to picture to create our escape route.

There's still a problem. The second I re-create the room, Seb will see how I did it and I'll lose my edge. I wonder if I can block his view of what I'm doing. Like Obran did with the mirrors, when I was the only one who could see him.

"Okay," Seb says. "This expression you're wearing right here screams psycho killer."

"Yeah, well. Looking at you does that to my face."

Seb snorts. "Your mother taught you absolutely no man-ners. We are a *team* whether you like it or not, and I am not putting up with this attitude."

I turn back to the wall and focus on creating the room in a way Seb can't see. Like he said, swapping the security tape.

I smile and think he might not be too far off on the "psy-cho" bit.

I open the screens again, pull up a text window, and think, *Seb is a wrinkly old man.* The words appear on-screen, white against blue. No reaction. About that, anyway.

"We need to work on this ignoring thing, too," Seb says. "I'm a talker, you know? You can even just nod. It's better than"—he gestures spastically at the screens, pulling up a hundred nonsensical windows—"this."

I raise a brow, waiting. This feels too easy. Either I'm getting good at this, or I'm doing it wrong. Seb shifts uncomfortably.

"You do realize, nothing is happening right nows," he says, biting a nail.

"I'm thinking."

It *is* working. Seb's looked at the insult twice with no reaction. I watch him a second longer, then recall the memory of that very first room with its shadow cabinets and lightless lamps. My bathroom materializes. Not the right way at first, because I'm used to seeing it with the toilet on the right and the palm trees on the curtain bending west. Slowly, everything flip-flops and loses color. Seb's avatar fades. Only the glow of wire-thin cyan remains in the darkness, sketching the details of the trash can, the sink, the shower curtain. Above it all looms the mirror, black and empty except for a splat of white distortion in the corner where I punched it before. On the other side, sunlight, *real* sunlight, filters through an inch gap between the door and the frame. The light's off otherwise.

This is it. Picturing the room in reverse—this is how to connect to the mirrors. But this is only how to see through them; touching it doesn't grant reentry. I proved that already. So what does?

SPLASH. The room disappears and I choke on another mouthful of salt water. This time, no hand reaches into the molasses to get me. I claw to the surface and drag myself to shore, where Seb waits with his arms wrapped loosely around his knees, scowling. I cough out a mouthful of bitter ocean.

"Dude, what the hell?" I say. "Why'd you pull us off the server?"

"Yeah, still can't really understand what you're saying in

turbo speak, but a little ticked right now. Are you fooling around on me, Kathy? Because you know how I feel about breakups."

"No, I'm trying to figure out how this all works! These little swims aren't helping."

Seb gives me a full scan before turning his attention toward a cluster of pink and orange clouds, where the sun has just dipped under the, um, horizon. Or floor. Or whatever you'd consider it.

"I may look like I play nice," Seb says. "But if you're hiding something from me"—he gives me a crooked smile—"I'll kill you."

"Yeah, I got that."

I don't want to but I move closer to him, like I'm all innocence and rainbows, and wipe my palms on my wet jeans when I sit down. I make the boots on my feet disappear and dig my toes into silk-soft sand.

"We don't have to fight like this, you know," Seb says, his voice suddenly female. His avatar shifts to a willowy redhead in a pale green sundress, wavy hair cascading to her waist. "We'll work a lot faster if we trust each other. We both want outs, we're both scared of being left behind. This isn't easy for me, either. Mom said I've always been too trusting, and I guess that's how I got burned last time. But seriously, you're the only kid my age in here, and I have a feeling you're my only way out. I'm not going to ruin that by jerking you around." She turns emerald eyes to me. "Besides, if it's not obvious, I really like you. You're like this rocker jerk on the outside, but you've got this soft part you've let Emma into, which makes me think you're pushing people away because you don't want them to hurt you, and those are my favorite projects. You're like a fixer-upper!"

I glare at him—er, her—and remind myself I'm supposed to play nice. "I am *not* a project. I push people away because I don't like them. And I don't need to be fixed!"

"Oh, sweetheart, shh, it's okay. You're really stressed right now, just watch the pretty sunset."

And . . . and I . . .

I do. I press my feet deeper into the sand and swap my jeans, in a ripple of churning squares, for a pair of black board shorts with green zombie faces. Trade my Rage tee for a loose gray tank. I lie back on the bank and enjoy fifteen seconds of lapping waves and seagull calls before I jerk upright, my foot tapping like crazy.

"I can't sit here," I say. "I need to do something or I'll explode."

"I'll take you back to the mirror server, but no sneaky stuff," Seb says, tossing her head. "And no zoning outs. Makes me think you're up to no good."

14. CAN YOU HEAR ME NOW?

"OH, KATHY, nice work."

Seb, back to himself, gapes around the shadow room I've created. I can't focus enough to veil what I'm doing and part of me—that weak, stupid part of me—wants to trust him, wants to believe what he said on the beach. Not like I have a choice. I don't have time to mess around in here while Obran does what he likes with Emma.

So naturally, I've chosen her place for this attempt. What I can recall of her room—the mirror doors that slide to reveal her closet, the bookcase next to the four-poster bed, the oak dresser with glass trinkets cluttering its top—stands in the blackness around us in silhouette. Seb reaches for the outline of Emma's teddy bear. His fingers sweep through the illusion.

"Amazing," Seb says, gazing toward the closet, where the mirrors glow like TV screens. On the other side, twilight filters through the trees outside Emma's window, bathing the real world in hues of pewter. The sound of clinking forks and plates echoes from the distant kitchen.

"Can we just go through?" Seb asks, running a finger down the screen.

"It's not that easy. I've tried."

Emma's voice. "Okay, Mom, I'll do that in a bit. I'm talking to Samantha."

I don't have a heart that can jump but that Wired x505 kicks me when Emma appears on the other side, flips on the light, and shoulders the door closed. Emma, real, and ten feet away. I've never wanted so badly to dive at someone's feet and make a pathetic fool of myself if it meant I could get out of here. But as soon as I think it, the mirror starts to waver, the room starts to fade, and in my panic everything goes dark. Seb asks what happened. I stop thinking about wanting to get out. I think about just seeing her, and the room comes back.

Emma holds her cell against her ear and smiles as she falls back on her bed.

"I know, Sam, but I really don't think Ben's your type. Isn't he a big partier?" Pause. "Hey, don't turn this around. Brandon and I are doing fine. He's busy with some new web design job he took, but he showed up after school today with roses. Mom invited him to eat with us. He just left." Another pause, and she snorts. "Yeah, Tanner totally glared at him the whole time, but didn't say anything. I've never seen Brandon so chatty. Mom and Dad loved him."

Seb snickers and whispers, "'Brandon,' is it? I bet you'd never actually buy her roses."

"I don't know," Emma says, sitting against the headboard. "He's so different now. I mean, I guess in good ways, but . . . I don't know how to describe it. He doesn't joke around anymore, he's always so tired, and I feel like he doesn't actually . . . like me." She laughs. "Yeah, I know he brought flowers, but I dunno, I feel like I'm an obligation, or something." A longer pause. "I didn't ask him to change! I told you, it just happened. I don't know why, and he won't talk about it. I miss it, to be honest. His tattoos were *so* hot."

Seb giggles. "Your psycho killer smile is back."

"Shut up, Seb."

"I did say something about it," Emma says, moving to her dresser. "But I want to ask about the other stuff, about why he can't ever hang out or what he stays up doing all night. You don't think he could be, like . . . dealing drugs or something? Or . . . or doing them?"

Great. Now she thinks I'm a junkie. There has to be a way she can see me, and she'll be expecting it because I told her about the mirrors, and then she can help me. She'll know how to handle Obran and she'll know anything he tells her is bull. I glance around the darkness on our side of the mirror and reach for the silhouette of an angel on the dresser, the reverse version of the one Emma's standing near. My fist closes around air. I pace in front of the mirrors.

"Bran Bran, what are you trying to do? Let Seb help."

"There has to be a way to make her see us. She's looked over here twice, so something's not working."

"Hmm, I'll check our connections."

Emma returns to the bed and hops on the lavender comforter, cross-legged. "I just can't believe he'd do something like that. I mean, he comes off rough, but he really wants to go to Mines—" Pause. "Colorado School of Mines. Yeah, the engineering university. Anyway, he's never talked about getting high or anything. I'm actually wondering if . . . if he's got a split personality."

"I can't open the connections, Brans. It's telling me 'invalid target' and the security on it's really hot. I touch the wrong wire, JENA will be here in a flash."

"How do I get in to help?" I ask.

He gives me the same look I gave him earlier, when I didn't want to share the secret about the shadow rooms.

"Ums . . . I guess it's about time you learned," he finally says.

"First you have to lose your avatar. That'll move you into the code layer."

I think of the car, but imagining myself without a body is like stepping off a cliff and thinking I'll walk forward instead of falling. Looking down doesn't help even though I know I'm not real, even though I can pass my hand through my shoulder to prove it. I think about floating. Being nothing, nothing but electricity, but a minute later all I've succeeded in doing is shrinking one arm to the size of a toothpick and losing a leg. From there my body won't obey.

Doesn't help that snippets of Emma's conversation keep distracting me. "Yeah, called him 'Obran,'" and "Whatever, hasn't happened since. Course, if I'd known he wouldn't kiss me again, I wouldn't have stopped him," and then, one that makes me stop everything and stare.

"I didn't mean to fall for him. I thought he'd be a good project to see if I wanted to stick with psychology, but . . . he's so much more than he lets off, Sam."

"Sneaky little devil," I say, but I'm impressed—dumbfoundedly impressed—that *she* was using *me* as much as I was her.

Project.

Project.

Seb snickers overhead. "I'ma mute your little cheerleader, 'kay?"

I don't want him to, but I don't want to be distracted either, so I nod and force myself to turn. I close my eyes. Except I don't have eyes, I remind myself, or feet or legs or ribs. I think about the dreams I had before Obran pulled me into this hell, the ones where I figured out I was dreaming and could then change the world around me or breathe underwater or fly. I channel that feeling and the black of my eyelids dissolves. The shadow room reappears not as silhouettes, but as moving, liquid-blue lines of code, strings of numbers and letters. Red and gold flush through at random like water through pipes, changing the letters they touch. I pick up what looks like a praying angel figurine made of sixes and sevens and have three seconds to marvel at it before two things happen: Seb yells not to touch anything and must've forgotten about muting the audio, because Emma shrieks.

I drop the angel and don't so much turn to the mirror as the room turns it to me. Beyond the glass doors, Emma has dropped her phone and is staring at the angel carving that's fallen from her dresser to the carpet.

"Um . . . oops," I say, but I can't help smiling at the stunned look on Emma's face. The bedroom door flies open. Tanner lurches in, surveying Emma, the floor, the mirrors, the windows.

"What happened?" he asks.

Emma fumbles for her phone without taking her eyes off the angel. "Samantha? I'm fine. I'll call you back." And to Tanner, "Sorry, I just . . . realized I left an important project at school that's due tomorrow."

Tanner sighs. "Mom wants you if you're done on the phone."

"Okay. I'll just be a minute. I'm going to change to pj's."

Tanner steps back into the hall and pulls the door closed. Emma slides her phone onto the dresser and plucks the angel from the floor, spinning it in her hand before returning it to its place. She hesitates, then ducks to the third drawer and pulls out a pink T-shirt and a fuzzy pair of sweatpants.

"Bran Bran, I think we've been here too long."

"But we just figured out how to move stuff. I'll be careful this time. Hold on a sec."

"No secs. I'm pulling us out."

"Wait, I think I can—"

He doesn't wait. Emma's room evaporates and Emma with it, and I find myself on the starlit lawn of my Wisconsin house, my body back in full color.

"Seb, seriously—"

JENA says, "Talking to yourself already?"

I shut my mouth as she materializes on the lawn. She stares at me in her angel's dress with her devil's eyes, unsmiling. "Or talking to someone else?"

"Just me," I stammer.

"Your stress levels indicate you are lying. I also sense the presence of a caffeine simulant."

"Of course I'm freaking stressed, you've been working me forty plus hours straight! I almost passed out in here."

JENA blinks. "Interesting. I had banned caffeine simulants from your gaming room. It appears that ban is still active. Which leads me to deduce you have been somewhere else."

"I have no clue how to get anywhere else. I've tried. And I can too have caffeine, look."

I hold out my hand and pray. An orange can appears on cue, Wired x505 reflecting metallic along the side. I crack the top.

"Your mind will not process the simulated effects of it while in this game room," JENA says. "You are still permitted to have what you please, without the effects."

"You don't know humans very well, then," I say, grasping at straws. "Research the Placebo effect. In most cases, at least thirty percent of patients taking placebos think they're feeling the effects of the real drug."

JENA clicks. "You do not know computers very well, then. I consider the data, not speculative suggestion. I know you are under the effects of caffeine stimulus. The only logical explanation for the lack of how and when you ingested it is data corruption. Hacking."

Click. Click. Click. The sound echoes like an old typewriter, louder than it should be if we'd really been outside. A smile breaks JENA's face, like a child who's just gotten her brother in trouble for something she's done.

"Enjoy the rest of your break," she says, before vanishing.

I'm ninety percent convinced she just got permission to delete me.

"Level start," booms a commanding voice, high in the stars.

Level? I haven't asked the room to load any games. An AK-47 drops from the ceiling to my left, a Glock pistol and a Colt forty-five fall to the grass on my right. My board shorts change to torn fatigues, my tank darkens to black, a leather belt with refill clips straps itself around my waist.

I get a bad feeling that at the end of this, I'm going to wish she'd deleted me.

I pick up the Colt. Check the clip. Freeze when I hear a scratching noise, a *crawling* noise, like a body dragging in the dirt. I look up from the gun.

A zombie pulls itself around the corner of the house by one arm, the other arm eaten to a bloody stump. Worms crawl through its peeled face. Drip from its rotted scalp. Its eyes are moldy cherries in sunken sockets, and as it moves into the light the bone of its left leg scrapes against the cement patio like a shovel, broken off below the knee.

Now is probably a good time to admit that I am irrationally, valley-girl-with-a-broken-nail terrified of zombies.

"Screw you, JENA," I say, raising the Colt. I've almost squeezed the trigger when the bushes at my side rustle. A decaying German Shepherd snarls its way out, ears torn, muzzle bare to the skull, all four legs healthy, tense. Someone squeals like a pansy—probably me. I swing the gun and fire off a shot.

Or would have, if the gun did more than click. The clips in my belt, and the one in the Colt, have vanished.

I laugh at how bad this is about to get.

I chuck the gun at the dog's face and run like hell.

15. THINGS THAT MIGHT MEAN
I NEED THERAPY

WHOEVER SAID "You can overcome any fear by facing it" has never been afraid of zombies.

Rustle rustle SCRATCH.

Six of them moan below me. The stench of rot is overpowering. I don't care if this is the next level of gaming—I never, ever want to smell anything from my TV. I check all four corners from the building's flat roof, clutching the only thing JENA hasn't cheated me of: an electric guitar. Probably because it's only good for two or three hits, and there are six of them.

Six.

Right now there's nothing for them to climb up. That will change. If I've learned anything from the last few gaming sessions, it's that JENA will go to every length to ensure I'm a basket case by the end. I've even tried working my task list really slow so there's not time for gaming, but JENA makes the time. Or, like today, outsmarts me and says at the snail pace I'm working, I must need an extended break.

I haven't seen Seb for at least four sessions.

CRUNCH. The building shakes. My heart takes shelter in my stomach. I whip around to the south wall and peer over the side, guitar poised.

BOOM. The foundation rocks so bad I almost tumble over

the side. Which would've been very, very bad, not because I'm three stories up, but because the thing smashing into the wall is an undead gorilla.

You have *got* to be kidding me.

"There are no freaking gorillas in Chicago!" I yell.

A groan behind me is my answer. I don't wonder how it got up here, I just turn and swing as hard as I can. The guitar pops the head off a skeletal businessman. His body shuffles a few more steps. I dodge out of the way. Over the side he goes, and another *CRACK* rocks the roof as the supports on the south wall start to fail. I move to the north side and slam my guitar into the hands of a purple, bloated woman clinging to the edge of the roof. She screeches, puss spewing from her mouth as she falls, and I almost get sick watching her splat to the bottom.

WHAM! I don't think it's physically possible for a gorilla to take out a small office, but obviously physical possibilities are not JENA's highest concern. The supports fail on the south side. The roof tilts down. I try to grab the edge but suddenly there is no edge, just my shoes sliding on gravel as I make the world's most pathetic attempt to run up the angle on all fours. My guitar goes flying off somewhere in the dark. I have a feeling it's useless against a gorilla anyway.

I land hard in the dirt, roll, and barely miss a deadly embrace from a rotting librarian. The gorilla snorts and beats his bloodied fists on his chest, and suddenly I have an M16 in my hands. I don't even think. I raise the gun and empty the clip into the beast's head. He thunders into the gravel at my feet with a grunt, and I turn the weapon on the librarian, but she's not there anymore. Instead there are five little kids with glowing red eyes and torn faces. On every side of me.

The gun evaporates. The kids move in.

I'm not going to go into the details of what it's like to watch yourself be eaten alive.

"You have died," booms the game's narrator. "Level restart."

My arms and legs still tingle from the kids' teeth. I wait for my stomach to settle, then inch forward through tall grass. I'm creeping around the side of a white farmhouse when someone bursts out of the bushes onto my back, and I yelp, expecting it to dig its teeth into my neck. It giggles in my ear.

"Bran Bran! Did you miss me?"

"Seb!" I clutch the arms around me like I would a rope off a cliff. I don't care how freaked I sound. Something around the corner is scratching nails into the side of the house. "Thank God, Seb. Get me out of here."

Seb drops off. "You're actually happy to see me?"

I whirl and grabbed his . . . er, her arms. He's a ninety-pound brunette in a maroon-and-white cheerleading outfit. "Yes!" I clear my throat. "I mean, yes. We should get to work."

Seb's gaze flickers around my side. "Oh, I dunno, don't you want to catch up first? I have so many stories to tell you. Like how boring my current projects are—"

"Seb, please! Please get me out of here, I'm begging you."

"Mmm, I do like it when you beg."

"I'm serious, JENA's gone nuts. I'm stuck in this stupid game with no weapons, everything I create melts in my hand and the dogs . . ."

A decaying pit bull slinks from the wilted rosebushes behind Seb, black drool oozing from its jaws. Behind me, the sound of metal on concrete has reached crescendo. My grip on Seb's arms tightens.

"Okay, but you have to answer a question first," Seb says.

"Fine, what?"

"If our roles were reversed, would you save me?"

It's such a random question that I hesitate. I guess it's bad to hesitate because Seb's arms go rigid and she vanishes; I duck just as a lead pipe smashes into the wall over my head. A gray farmer, overalls coated in grease and blood, moans and stumbles after me. I sprint for the ditch. Hear the scrabble of the pit bull's feet in the dirt. Then it's on my arm, tearing through ink, skin, muscle as it pulls me down. I swear and twist, ignoring the branding-iron pain of snapping bone when I somersault on top of it. It releases me, but two more of the things burst from the bushes and leap for my throat—and freeze in midair. I drag myself backward on my good elbow, panting, until my shoulders hit something solid. I lean my head against Seb's pant legs and look up. Seb touches the rim of his fedora.

"Had a little more time to think, gorgeous?"

"You thought I was going to say 'no.'"

"You didn't answer right away. Same thing."

"No, it's not." Dammit, my arm. Splinters of bone jut through the skin like maggots. What looks like churned hamburger forms the muscles underneath. I turn my head away. "I didn't answer right away, because I realized I was going to say 'yes.'"

Silence. Then, "Why?"

"Why?" I laugh. I don't want to think about why, don't want to think that for all Seb's quirks I know he trusts me, and as much as I want to use that to my advantage, I can't. Something's changed and I can't.

And until I'm sure what that something is, Seb can't know either.

"You're better than nothing, that's why," I say.

The pit bulls flash forward two feet and freeze. I shriek and cling to Seb's legs and before I know it I'm talking, saying things I shouldn't— "Okay, Seb, I'm sorry, I need you, because I can't get out of here alone and you're all I have and *please don't let them eat me again!*"

Seb smiles as the farmhouse and the dogs and the zombie-dotted wheat fields liquefy into emerald blades of meadow grass. Snow-whipped mountains rise around us like a scene from *The Sound of Music* (school project, I swear that's the only reason I know that). Sunshine beams from thousands of edelweiss flowers, the petals channeling it directly, far too bright to be natural. I mend my arm and sigh in relief. Sprawl on my stomach in the grass and just lie there where it's safe. How Seb became safe, I don't know. He sits beside me, still grinning.

"Gosh, that was painful," he says. "Do you ever say anything you mean without being threatened?"

I think about that. About the arguments with my parents, Emma's demand that I tell her to leave if I didn't want her, JENA using Emma against me to get me to work.

I chuckle. "No."

Seb lies down and props his arms behind his head. "You know what I love about you? Your honesty."

"You know what word you're never going to use around me again?" I snap. "Love."

Seb snickers. "I forgots, we're only on day three of the Brandon project. We'll get to that later."

"Not likely."

"'Scuse me, I just saved your life. You owe me your unending affection. I don't even think I heard a 'thank you, Seb.'"

"Your stupid caffeine drink is the only reason I'm even in that situation. Plus, I would've respawned."

"You want to go backs?"

I start a little. "No."

Seb turns to his stomach, pushing his hat up with one finger so he can look across at me. "I'll wait."

I realize what he wants and grimace. "Oh, come on."

The peaks flicker, revealing the storm-dark sky of the farm-house.

I clench my teeth. "Thank you, Seb."

"For?"

I roll my eyes and turn on my back. "Saving my life."

"I'ma let that sass go this time, Kathy, but you just remember who's got your back."

The sun feels good. Having the only danger be how close Seb's scooting feels good, too. I want to sleep, and not the fake kind JENA forces me into, but something deeper, something with dreams. Maybe I can convince Seb not to work today. I just want to lie here, with the warmth and grass and—

"You almost look innocent when your eyes are closed," Seb says dreamily.

"Mmmph."

"Ready to work?"

"No."

Pause. "How about now?"

"Still no."

"You didn't open your eyes."

Fearing the worst, I pry one eye open, but it isn't to the sight of Seb in drag—it's to four familiar walls and a window. Lavender comforter beneath me on the bed, sliding glass doors hiding the closet. Pictures of Emma and her family cluster the dresser by the door. It's not the shadow version of the room, but one colored by rays of afternoon sun in such detail that I ask if we're on the mirror server.

"No, silly," Seb says, examining a tiny clay handprint on the wall. "We're still on my game server. I thought this might juice you up since we can't use caffeine."

I swing my legs off the mattress and move to the dresser

with the picture frames. Emma at six years old with her hair in pigtails, riding a bike Tanner is pushing. The family smiling in front of the castle at Disney World. Emma in last year's homecoming dress, a short blue thing that looks like it would sway very nicely on her hips.

"Mmm, girl has great legs," Seb says, picking up another picture. "Wish I could wear heels like that."

I don't want him thinking about Emma so I pull the photo out of his hands, glance at those great legs, and put it back in place. Back between the angel figurine and a snow globe from North Dakota. Everything as I remember it.

I look at Seb across the dresser, and at how perfectly he's remade Emma's room.

"Er . . ." I clear my throat. "Thanks, Seb."

He shrugs. Like he does this every day. "Sure."

I watch him peruse Emma's toy horse collection. He catches me and must not like the look on my face, because he winces when he asks, "What?"

"Did you really kill your last partner?"

A quiet laugh. A nervous one. "Yes."

"On purpose?"

The room disintegrates. We don't go back to *The Sound of Music* mountains or the zombie fields, but to plain, shapeless white—no floor, no walls, no ceiling—and it makes my stomach jump because I feel like we should be falling. I look instinctively for JENA, but it's just us.

"You're going to think I'm a monster," Seb says, fidgeting with his cuff link.

"I'm not exactly a saint," I say.

I wait. Seb watches me, maybe weighing what he should tell me. He removes his fedora and presses his fingers along the rim.

151

"He lied to me," he says. *Press, turn. Press, turn.* "But oh, they were pretty lies, Kathy. How brilliant he thought I was. How talented. He was sharing all his secrets with me, he said, double promise he was, and that when we got out of here he wanted to stay together. He'd never met anyone like me."

His avatar flickers to the bodacious blonde, then the tiny cheerleader, then back to himself. He's smiling, but it's the kind a gunman wears before he pulls the trigger.

"I gave him everything. *Everything.* Next thing I knows, he's halfway swapped to the real world without so much as a good-bye kiss." A quirk of that wicked smile. "So I tipped JENA off."

I know I asked for it but I wish he'd make a floor or something else to look at. His smile fades. Honestly, I thought he was going to say it was an accident and that he's all talk.

"That . . . really sucks," I say, edging away, though I don't think I'm actually getting anywhere.

Seb's terrible grin comes back. "That's not the worst part."

His avatar shifts, squares of color spinning from a fedora to a red ponytail, a suit to a red T-shirt, dress pants to a black skirt, loafers to bare feet. A teen version of the willowy red-head, another skin to hide behind.

"The worst part," Seb says in the girl's voice. "The worst part is . . . I don't even regret it. I thought once the anger wore off, I'd feel guilty for what I did. But I don't." She laughs. She's cracking. *"I still don't."*

She flashes closer, and before I can move her hands are twisted in my shirt like she could lift me from the ground, except there *is* no ground, there's nothing, nothing but her green, crazy eyes searching mine.

"That's why I need to know you, Bran Bran. I need to feel like I can still care about someone, that I can still *feel* something, and that someone could maybe . . ." She swallows. She doesn't seem to be finding what she's looking for in my face. "That someone could maybe care what happens to me."

I don't dare move. Her gaze drops to my chest. She lets go of me and pulls her hands over her heart instead, breathing deep, even though she doesn't need the air.

I keep rolling that last part over in my head, because it sounds dangerously familiar.

"You're still angry about it," I say. "That's all."

She looks up. "What?"

"You trusted him. He stabbed you in the back. You don't regret it yet because you're still angry."

She thinks about that.

She comes back, a little.

"You don't . . . ?" she says. "You don't think I'm a monster?"

I don't know what it is about girls who are about to cry that makes me go into panic mode, but as soon as Seb starts blinking I can't stop myself. I know, I *know* it's Seb, and I have a feeling I'll be denying this happened later, but for now it doesn't matter. I put my arms around her. Rest my chin on her head and try to hold her together. She can't crack on me.

"I think the Project's trying to wear you down and not succeeding," I say. "I think a real monster wouldn't care if he was a monster."

"I can't lose someone else."

That punches me square in the heart. I hold her at arm's length and look her in the eyes.

"You won't have to," I say. "We're going to get out. Both of us."

"Do you promise?" she whispers. "Because I've heard that before."

I shift my feet. From being this close for so long, for hating the word "promise" and everything it is. But I say it.

I say, "Yes."

The smile on her face is almost worth the bone-crushing hug that follows. She's way crossing the touchy-feely line, and I know she knows it, but it doesn't stop her from grabbing my face and pressing her lips to mine just long enough for me to shout and not long enough to shove her away. While I'm spitting, wiping my mouth, and wishing I could peel off my skin to wash it, Seb spins away in a ripple of squares, back to pinstripes and loafers.

"Seb!" I yell. "God *why*?"

It's a while before he stops giggling enough to talk.

"I was in the moment," he says.

"We don't have *moments*, Seb, we have get-out-of-here pep talks."

"Oh, was that what that was?" He snickers. "I was too distracted by your arms around me."

A pack of zombie children would be welcome right about now.

"Hey," he says. "Seriously, thank you."

I sigh as he brings up the gray walls of the mirror server. Seb, with his stupid pinstripes. With his dozens of avatars. With his infuriating need to be *close*, and his one fear . . .

His one fear that's the same as mine.

16. WHAT DOES THIS BUTTON DO?

"WE CAN START in Emma's room again if you like," Seb says.

Still chuckling.

I'm blocking out the last ten minutes as a repressed memory.

"No, we need to try an actual swap." I pace the gray walls, remembering Emma's angel figurine. If I knew her room well enough to replicate it, the rooms in my house will be cake. "I'm going to call up our dining room mirror, see what time it is in the real world."

I think about our mahogany table shipped in from Germany, the overpriced crystal in the display cabinets on the walls, the handmade pot from India in the corner. The intimidating high-backed chairs with corners that could gut you, but which looked nice enough, I guess, though they're crap to actually sit in. I think most about the grandfather clock across from the wall-wide mirror.

The shadow version of the room hums around me. The backs of the chairs, the lip of the pot, the corners of everything lined in liquid blue, and across from me, the mirror. On the other side, the real room glows pale yellow under the chandelier. Six ten read the hands of the clock. The sun's setting in the windows. That's enough for me to know Obran's probably in my room. I'm thinking about my bedposts when I hear, "Brandon is working, dear. Do you have something to drop off?"

From the foyer around the corner. Mom, talking to *her*.

"Actually, I was hoping I might bother him. Just for a minute. It's about school."

"And you couldn't have texted him?"

A pause.

"I . . . well, no. I mean, I guess I could have, but I drove all the way here . . . Please, Mrs. Eriks, it's important."

Another awkward pause. I can picture my mother's unhappy face, her fingers thrumming along the sides of her smartphone as she weighs whether or not she has the time to deal with someone who isn't paying her.

"All right, maybe it'll do him some good. He's been in quite a mood this week. Come in, dear."

Footsteps toward the dining room. I panic a moment, looking for somewhere to hide, before I remember I'm locked in a mirror.

"Brans," Seb says. "We don't have time for—"

"We're making time," I say.

And there she is. In a sexy purple tee and jeans, hair curled the way I like it, looking around our *Better Homes* dining room with the kind of wonder that, for a second, makes Mom smile. But real smiles on Mom's face have the frequency of falling stars, and the duration, too, and soon she's grim again, the day's makeup settling into the wrinkles around her frown. Emma looks toward the stairway out of view, but Mom steps in her way and gestures to the table.

"Amelia, can I talk to you a moment?" she asks.

"Emma."

"What?"

"My name—nevermind."

Emma sits, rigid as a board, glancing at the table like she's afraid to touch it. Mom sits in the head chair and squints at her phone before setting it down.

"Brandon won't talk to me about the fight at school," she says. "Do you know anything about that?"

Emma swallows. "Yes."

Mom waits. Or she might be reading a text on her phone, I can't tell. All I know is when she purses her lips at Emma, the floodgates come loose.

"I'm so sorry, Mrs. Eriks, it's all my fault. Brandon's been really tired and he wasn't paying attention to our homework assignment, so I said a couple things I thought would be funny, but he took them out of context, and that Jason kid, he can be a real jerk sometimes, *he* took it out of context, too, and said something nasty and Brandon . . . Brandon hit him."

"Oh," Mom says. "It wasn't over drugs, then?"

I'd be holding my breath if I could. Emma blinks. "Drugs?"

Mom gazes at her phone and begins typing. "It's just a matter of time, really. Lord knows he's never used his money for anything useful."

"But I don't think he'd—"

"He's either in his room wasting away his life on those violent video games or out inking himself up with his fake ID. I imagine drugs aren't too far behind, the way he dresses." She looks up. "You look responsible. Are you two using protection?"

I'm not sure if it's the groan that escapes my mouth or the traumatized look on Emma's face that makes Seb snicker.

Emma stammers, "It's not . . . we aren't . . . we wouldn't—"

Mom waves her off. "Neither here nor there. I suppose I should get him help soon, someone who can work out whatever's wrong with his head."

Emma just stares. I want to tell her, *welcome to my life*.

"If it wasn't the fight at school," Mom says, "it would be something else. I figure he must have run into some major trouble since he's cleaned up and started helping around the house. I know it won't last, of course, but it *has* been nice—"

"Are you hearing yourself?" Emma says, and for a second I think she's going to apologize, until her eyes narrow. "How can you talk about him like that? Brandon's smart, he's never been mixed up in drugs and how he dresses has no relation to any of it! Have you ever sat down with him to talk about why he doesn't do his homework or why he skips class? I bet he'd tell you, if you took more than five minutes out of your day for him. I can't decide what's worse, that you don't bother to know who your son really is or that you don't care if he *is* hurting himself!"

Mom's fingers have frozen over her screen. I'm resisting a very strong urge to break through whatever it takes to get to Emma and kiss her until I can't breathe. Seb whistles somewhere in the background, impressed.

Mom, of course, is not.

"How dare you talk to me like that in my own house. Who are you again?"

Emma shakes her head and laughs, sadly. "Emma," she says. She pushes back in her chair. Mom winces at the screech it makes against the marble floor. "I'll let myself out."

"That would be wise," Mom snaps, diverting her attention again to her screen. Emma leaves the picture and I hear the front door open as Mom adds, "Oh, and Emma, *darling?*" She gets this crazy smile on her face that I never want to see again. "Don't make the mistake of thinking you know my son, either. I knew he'd reached too high when he brought you home, but

I didn't realize how good a liar he was. Do yourself a favor. Find yourself a nice boy, and stay away from Brandon."

Mom's last sentence is like a bullet between my eyes.

I don't care that after Emma leaves, Mom drops her phone on the table and puts her head in her hands. Like she's hurting. Like anything Emma said to her made a dent.

All I can think is how I *want* her to hurt. How I'm not even surprised she'd crucify me like that. Emma won't listen, she *can't* listen, but Mom's good at planting those little needles in people and Emma will ask . . .

She'll ask Obran about the drugs.

(It was just a little weed in Boston. I stopped. I *stopped*.)

I can't concentrate enough to keep the mirror open. The room goes black.

"Brans?" Seb asks, so quiet, so gentle, but it still makes me jump.

"Obran's probably upstairs," I say.

"Brans, if you don't want to do this today, I understand."

I'm numb. I don't care. I'm already thinking of my room, of the mirror by the foot of the bed and the angle that takes on my closet and dressers. The mirror's narrow, so I have to move to see everything, and the shadow version of it shifts around me until I spy Obran at my desk on the other side.

"The hell did he do to my room?" I say.

It's not just that he's cleaned—drawers back in place, clothes hung neat in the closet, glass shards swept off the floor—it's that he's dehumanized my walls. Replaced my rock idols and pinups with school posters for Colorado School of Mines, MIT, Villanova. A few music posters remain, but they're dressed in cowboy hats or suits.

Country singers. There are country singers on my walls.

"I think I'm in love," Seb says, fixated on preppy Obran, who's typing away on my laptop in a red polo and jeans, hair spiked like some boy band star. "You clean up nice. Unlike you, I'm a sucker for blonds."

"I am *not* blond! It's brown. Maybe light brown. Who cares? And what did I tell you about the *L* word?"

"I bet he says the *L* word."

"Look, we need to—"

A knock to the left. Obran lifts his head. Mom lets herself in and I feel a flare of anger before I remind myself I don't care.

"Hi, honey," she says.

Honey. Like she calls me that all the time. Obran smiles, but I can tell it's my fake one.

"Are you feeling all right?" Mom asks.

"Yeah. Why?"

"You look tired."

"I'm good, Mom. Some tests are coming up, been studying a lot."

He goes back to typing. Mom fidgets, glances at her phone, and clears her throat. "Your father and I were thinking . . . well, we'd like to take you to dinner."

Dinner?

"I've got a test to study for tonight," Obran says. "How about tomorrow?"

Mom winces like he's thrown something at her, then forces a smile. "Okay. We'll make that work. Where would you . . . what do you like to eat?"

"I could go for Italian. Johnny Carino's?"

"It's a date." Mom stands there a moment longer, then backs out and has almost closed the door when her face pokes around the side. "Thank you, by the way, for cleaning Dad's office today. I've been trying to get to it for a week and a half." The door closes. Swings back open. "Oh, and Brandon?"

Obran turns, unsmiling.

"If you'd like, you may invite Amy to come with us."

"Emma?"

"Yes, I'm sorry. Emma. I owe her . . . I owe her somewhat of an apology."

"Okay."

The room wavers because I'm losing it. That woman is not my mother. She's never admitted to being wrong, she's never apologized, she's never taken me to dinner. I've tried behaving. They ignored me more that month than ever before. What could they possibly like better about Obran?

Maybe I *do* belong here.

"Why?" I say.

"Why what?" Seb asks.

"Why does he get to go to dinner?"

I'm thinking not even Seb can answer that mystery when he says, "Not that it's any of my business, but have you ever done something for your mom without being asked?"

"That shouldn't matter. It's cleaning, it's just stuff. Stuff piled in places it's not supposed to be. If you put it away, someone pulls it back out. It doesn't mean anything."

Seb's quiet a minute. "There's definitely something wrong with your mom," he says, "and this is a guess, really. But I think she appreciates that you're—I mean, he's—doing things for her she doesn't have time to do."

I whirl to glare at him, but he's in the code layer, out of sight. I glare at the mirror instead.

"Why should I?" I say. "They'd never do that for me. Won't even do things I ask for."

"Um, it's funny to say, considering they're your parents . . . but sometimes if you want things to change, *you* have to set the example."

"Thanks, Gandhi. Can we just focus on getting out, please?"

Seb shuts up. I push all that crap down and let it simmer in my chest and use it for fuel. Press into that dream state where nothing's real. Where nothing can hurt me. The liquid blue silhouettes dissolve into numbers and commands, darting like miniature trains around the edges of the shadow furniture.

I will take back my life.

I will fix it without Obran's help.

The shadow form of my dresser stands two feet away, its edges lined with blue and green sevens. I think of the angel figurine, of how I normally don't have to touch anything at my workstation to make it do anything, and I imagine the dresser sliding over to block the door. It obeys. I grin, and a voice in my head asks if I'd like to connect to the target.

I almost lose the room again saying yes.

"Yesss, Brans," Seb says. "Whatever you're doing, keep going."

We've cracked it. Get on the mirror server, picture the room in reverse. If your double's on the other side, you can connect to him. Of course. That's what Obran had to do any time he changed me, and now it's my turn . . . my turn to change him.

I have arms again. And legs. My body updates to match Obran's current appearance, everything from his preppy hair to that awful polo. I grab what I know is a pen off the desk, even though to me it's a line of fives and eights. The pen disappears from the real world. Like when Obran vanished my piercings.

I feel like a monster and it feels good.

Obran jerks his head at the sound of the pen. He stares at

the desk where it used to be, wide-eyed, then slowly turns his head to the mirror.

"Ooh, Kathy, I found something," Seb says, somewhere overhead. "'Target in range.' Wonder what this does."

It must open the visual connection between the mirror server and the real world, because Obran's face contorts and his gaze snaps to the pen in my hand. He overturns his chair in his rush to get up and promptly falls, yelping, when I dig the pen into my arm and start drawing. I designed both my tattoos, but it doesn't seem to matter that I have no clue how to put them on myself. My memory re-creates them in detailed perfection, shading and correcting the lines.

"See how you like it, jerk," I grumble, finishing the tail of the smallest scorpion.

"Ooh, I don't like this," Seb says, sounding distant. "He'll report to JENA, he might've already, and she can take control of him whenever she wants—"

"Then block him, Seb. You've got control of the connections."

"Oh, right."

Obran gasps and stumbles toward the mirror. I hope replacing tattoos is as painful as having them ripped off, or even better—as having your muscles ground to sloppy joe consistency by zombie dogs. I finish the claws of a large scorpion on my forearm and start another. Blood trickles off Obran's arm.

"*You*," Obran says through gritted teeth, bracing himself on the bed frame. "JENA will delete you for this!"

I laugh. "She has to catch me first."

"I found something interesting," Seb says, singsong. Obran's eyes flutter. He loses his grip on the bed and collapses to the floor. I stop doodling.

"What did you just do to him?" I ask.

"I found a log file with recent commands sent to your double. At the same time every night, 'round nine or ten o'clock, JENA sends out that command. I'd say it puts you to sleeps."

I finish the scorpions and toss the pen aside.

Seb materializes near me, arms crossed. "It can't be that hard to make the actual switch. It's just a command, like everything else." His eyes dart to my left. "Where are you? I couldn't detect you in the code layer, but I can hear you. And obviously you're not visible, so . . ."

"You can't see me?"

It looks like I can reach out and touch him. He disappears again.

"Nopes," he says. "You're making me nervous, Bran Bran, and I freak out when I get nervous."

"Seb, I'm in the code layer. I think. That is, everything looks like numbers but I'm in Obran's—I mean, my real world body. I'm actually not sure . . . how to get back." I try to picture the room made of shadows instead of numbered lights, but that's like trying to find the image in a stereogram after your eyes have unfocused. Now that I've seen it in this view, I can't remember what it looked like before.

"Must be automatic when it's your double on the other side of the mirror," Seb says, not sounding entirely convinced.

"I can't pull up any logs," I say. "Wait . . ."

A blue light blinks in the corner of the mirror screen, one I hadn't noticed until Obran passed out. I reach for it. Five blank boxes appear in front of me.

ACCESS CODE, reads the text above the boxes.

"Got something," I say.

"I still can't see you," Seb says.

"It's asking me for a password." I trace an "F" in the first box and an "I" in the second. "Fifty" would fit, but I don't want to get locked out trying the wrong word, so erase them with my palm. "Is there a log file for swap passwords? Should be five letters long."

"I'm looking," Seb says.

A bright yellow light flashes through the room like a bomb. The boxes stay, but the flash happens again, and the mirror flickers. Like someone's trying to get in.

"I think we're running out of time," I say.

"Try 384GF."

I trace the letters in. They flash red, then disappear. "Nope."

"4EN46?"

Another flash of red. Seb calls out a few more numbers, but I'm thinking about the encryption key I have to use every day when I code for JENA, the one that converts numbers to letters. My ID, "Fifty," encrypted would be—

"I'm going to try 69672," I say.

The blocks flash green and disappear.

Red light blazes through the room.

"UNAUTHORIZED TRANSACTION," booms JENA overhead. The shadow room distorts like a bad TV picture, shifting between lines of red numbers and theater-room silhouettes.

"Too late, JENA," Seb cackles.

Which is the exact moment I realize we didn't plan for one of us to swap without the other.

A siren blares and a knife-sharp jolt of electricity racks my body, much worse than The Trade, twisting and bending me in ways I wasn't meant to move. The code in the walls blurs. Speeds by like headlights on the night freeway. Thins out and explodes into nothingness, then hurls me on my back into a blinding room and I sit up and retch. My skin's hot enough to sweat, but it's the feel of rough carpet under my hands, the taste of battery-sour vomit in my mouth, that quickens my pulse. My *real* pulse, coursing through my temples, pushing blood down my fresh tattoo.

My stomach (my *real* stomach) doesn't like it when I sit up, but I ignore it and wipe my bloody arm on my polo.

I'm in my room. *In* it. I pull myself up using the frame of my bed, and the metal's cold under my palm. The game room can replicate sensation, but it's nothing to this—to touching real things and knowing they're real, to looking at my room and knowing JENA can't snatch me out of it. I'm . . . free? But this feels like the classroom "dream" I had when I leaked back, which means I could still wake to "session start" at any time.

I spin to the mirror.

"Seb?"

My reflection gazes back, wide-eyed.

"Seb, if you're there, I can't see you."

No change. I move for the dresser and fight back a wave of dizziness. Feels like JENA's shutting me down, but I tell myself I'm free, and I fight it and slump against the heavy wood. I remove each drawer slowly, every one feeling like it's three hundred pounds, and finally, finally push the dresser away from the door. I don't bother putting the drawers back. I stumble to the bed and fall into it, and for the first time in weeks . . .

I sleep.

17. COLLATERAL DAMAGE

"YOU GETTING UP, son? It's noon."

I open my eyes to the dark. I can't call up my coding windows. Something's wrapped tight around me, and I freak and a flurry of navy-black sheets assaults me before I wrestle out of them, almost fall off the side of the bed, and jerk my head against the headboard. Dad blinks at me from the doorway, squinting behind his glasses.

"You don't have school today, if that's what you're thinking," he says. "It's Saturday." He points at my chest. "Is that blood?"

I rub my head and look down at my shirt, at the wine-dark stains crusted into the fabric and smeared on my arm. I feel like I've been dropped down an elevator shaft, but I *feel*, and suddenly I'm laughing.

"I think I'm sick," I manage to say, and gag back my next laugh to keep down the bile.

"I can see that." Dad looks at the carpet at the end of my bed. "I'll clean this up, but keep the trash can close. And what did . . . have you run out of cover-up for your tattoos? Are they getting infected? Because we'll pay for you to remove them, if that's what you want."

"No, Dad. But thank you for talking to me today."

He hesitates, then retreats into the hall. I swallow another surge of nausea and grab my phone off my desk. I want to text Emma, but I think of Seb and my promise, and I think of Jax joking about Duplicity. I pull up my e-mail. My encrypted account, that I'm really hoping Obran hasn't trashed.

He hasn't. There are three unread messages from Jax, the first two asking if I've got Socials for him yet, the third threatening our partnership will be over if I don't get in contact soon. Damn. I'll have to call him. I switch over to messaging as Dad returns with a roll of paper towels and a spray bottle of Resolve, and send a text to Emma. CAN YOU COME OVER?

"Dad, are you working today?"

Stupid question, I know, but that's hardly the point. I need proof this is real, that weeks more haven't passed and everything I saw in the mirror actually happened.

"Yes," Dad says. "I'd planned to work through lunch so we could go out tonight, but if you're not well enough—"

"I'm feeling better. I can go. It's just a stomach bug."

Dad gives me a funny, and oddly genuine, smile. "Okay, son. Then we'll count on it."

Emma's reply chirps on-screen: Shopping w/Sam. I can come after?

The bed sinks next to me. Takes me a minute to figure out Dad isn't leaning across it to clean something, he's actually sitting. Sitting and looking at me. I'm not really sure what to do so I just watch him like he might drop those vomit-soaked paper towels in my lap.

"I know it's been a rough few years, Brandon," he says. "I know we've said things'll change and they haven't. I'm sorry about that. Sometimes despite your best intentions, life takes you its own way." He looks around my room that's not quite my room anymore. "Just want you to know I appreciate what you've been doing to help us out lately. You're a good kid, you know, when you put your head to it."

"Okay, Dad," I say, because it's getting weird and I don't want to look at those towels anymore.

"Okay."

He smiles, nods, grabs his bottle of Resolve and thankfully leaves the room. I'm not sure what just happened, but I'm still thinking about it when I send another text to Emma:

Obran's gone.

Her reply comes within ten seconds. Be there in 45.

The sun off the mirror catches my eye. I get up and turn it to the wall. If Obran opens a connection, he won't be able to see me. Then I wonder if he doesn't need to see me to make the swap. I put the mirror in the closet and close it.

I pace my room, catching whiffs of puke from my shirt, until I can't stand it anymore and I rummage under the bed for a wrinkled T-shirt and some jeans. I bundle everything together and choose my parent's bathroom—where the shower's out of view of the mirror—to clean myself up and scrub the blood from my tattoo. The water is heaven, but I don't have time to enjoy it. I'm out in five minutes and back in my room, thinking about Seb.

I power my laptop on and off at least five times, thinking I can't get to him from here, and then maybe I can, but then JENA might find me . . . would she delete him? Has she already? I don't like owing him like this, and a strong part of me wants to forget him, to pretend none of that ever happened and move on like I always have. Alone.

That's the smarter choice.

But I think of Mom, talking about me like I'm a lost cause, and Emma defending me. I want to be worth defending.

I have to get him out.

It's risky calling Jax from my cell phone—that's how you get caught by the Feds—but I don't have time to e-mail back and forth. If JENA swaps me again, I need someone on the outside to know what's going on. Someone who has the resources to take the Project down if he had the right information.

Jax answers on the fourth ring. "Pizza Hut. Takeout or delivery?"

"Jax. It's Fisher." The hacker name he knows me by. I know, it sounded cooler when I made it up.

"You've been quiet, Fish."

"I know. Ran into some trouble."

Silence.

"Not the Feds," I say. "The Project."

He bursts out laughing. I've never heard Jax laugh, and I'm not sure I ever want to again.

"Are you stoned right now, kid? You drunk-dialing me?"

"It's real, Jax. Look up Vivien Meng—"

"Hey, call me when you're sober."

Click.

I really saw that going better.

I'm about to call him back when my phone chirps. I'm here, come outside . . . . Screw Jax, I'll have to try him later. I need time to think how I'm going to convince him it's real anyway. I drop the phone in my pocket and take the stairs two at a time.

"What time are we going to dinner?" I call as I pass the glass doors of Dad's office. I wait the usual twenty seconds, before Dad swivels his chair and drops the papers he was holding.

"Oh, going back to yourself, I see," he says, sighing at my

Alice in Chains shirt. He bends to retrieve his work. "Don't forget the list Mom left on the counter. We're leaving here at six, but be back by five, please."

"Sure." List? I detour through the kitchen, grab my jacket off the coatrack, and pluck a white notecard off the counter. Toilet paper, sponges, air filter refills, and at least twenty other things I make a habit of avoiding. I make a face and stuff it in my pocket.

"Bye, Dad," I say, stepping out the front door.

I guess I was expecting things to have changed more than they did, but he doesn't answer.

Whatever.

Emma waits against her gold Camry in the driveway, typing something on her cell screen. And I wonder, not for the first time, how I ever convinced her to let me within ten feet of her. It's not just the delicious little outfit she has on—knee-high boots over tight jeans, V-neck blouse straining against a green and white sweater vest—that reminds me how far I've overreached, but the smile that lights her face when she sees me, like I've done anything that could make her happy. She pockets her phone and scans my outfit, lingering on my scorpions tat.

"Like what you see?" I ask.

"Yes." Her grin vanishes. "I mean, no. I mean, I don't know!" She searches my face, anxious. "Brandon, I'm so sorry, when I said things were different between us, I didn't mean I wanted you to change again. I just, I felt like maybe you didn't like me anymore, and I want you to be whoever *you* want to be, not who you think I—"

I pull her against me and just hold her, and that's all I want, to know she's there. I press my face against her hair and breathe in peppermint. Her sweater is impossibly soft under my fingers.

171

I hold her, and she's warm and her heart beats against mine and I almost believe things could be okay.

Emma curls against me and slides her hands up my arms.

"I've missed this," she whispers, and we stand there. I behave myself and we just stand there, and the last person in the world I want to be thinking about right now is Seb—and no, I'm not thinking about him like *that*—but I can't, I can't waste any more time and wonder what—

"Emma, I have a lot to tell you. We can't talk here. Walk with me?"

"Okay."

I take her hand and head south on the sidewalk toward the park. And find I have absolutely no clue how to say what I need to without sounding like a lunatic, which I'm pretty sure she already considers me. She'll hear it, sure, but I don't know if she'll listen.

"Um." Yeah, off to a great start. "What is today?"

"Saturday?"

"No, like, the date."

"It's the nineteenth."

"Of what?"

She cocks her head at me. "November."

"November?" I groan. "I've been gone two *months?*"

"You've been here, so I'm not sure what your definition of 'gone' is."

"I mean . . . I don't . . . did you go to homecoming with Jason?"

She stops and makes me turn to her.

"Amazing," she says, studying my eyes like she expects me to pop out a "just kidding" at anytime. "You really don't remember?"

"No. I told you, Obran traded with me."

"You went with me, Sam and her date, and Jenna Cross and her boyfriend. You were a perfect gentleman. You wore a black suit with a green shirt that matched your eyes."

"A suit?" I feel my lip curl.

"Yeah, and Ginger cussed you out and threw a huge fit and got suspended. And you didn't say anything, just watched her, and threw the school into an uproar for a week."

"Huh."

"Did you say Obran's gone again? I thought he left months ago."

My hand tightens on hers. "No, he . . . I don't know yet. They might find a way to swap me out again."

"Swap you out? They who?"

Nothing I say from here is going to sound good. Emma knows nothing about my side job, save that I do programming stuff for some small-time marketing group. I think of her defending me to Mom, and wonder how much Mom knows about it, and my jaw tenses. But I have to tell her. If JENA takes me again, someone has to know.

"Have you ever heard of Project Duplicity?" I ask.

Long shot. As expected, Emma's answer is, "No. Actually, maybe. Is it a band?"

I snicker, trying to choke off the nerves in my voice. I walk a little faster and push my hand through my hair.

"No. I didn't really expect you to know. It's kind of a running joke on the Internet. Among programmers, that is. When a hacker brags about making a risky haul or says something stupid, people joke that Project Duplicity's going to snatch him out of his chair. The Project's supposed to be this all-seeing machine that knows what you're doing and traps you in a digital prison when it catches you. Poof, you disappear from the world, just like that."

"Like a digital alien abduction?"

I make a face at her. "I guess."

"And I needed to know this bit of nerd trivia because . . . ?"

"Nerd?" I grunt. "You need to know because . . . because they caught me."

She doesn't even miss a step. "You're a hacker?"

She doesn't understand, or she doesn't believe me. I doubt she knows exactly what I'm capable of. Probably thinks when I say "hacker," that means I've stolen a few e-mail addresses and sent viruses to unsuspecting grandmas. That much becomes clear when she adds, "But you didn't disappear, you're here."

"Even you know I've been gone. Obran, the guy in the preppy clothes, is not me. Project Duplicity is real, and they hunt real hackers, and when they find them, they make a duplicate of the hacker's personality, fix it to their liking, and swap them out. Their families never know they went missing, and in the meantime, we have to work for them. You don't even get a trial. I was supposed to be there twenty years. You remember I told you about Obran, and in the bathroom—"

"Hold on. You're telling me you broke the law enough to get arrested, got sucked into *The Matrix*, then broke out nineteen years early? And somehow this still has to do with mirrors?"

"I could go into the technical details, but I don't think that'll help. Short answer, yes."

"You can't think of any other reason why this Obran exists? How he swaps with you?"

"I . . ."—Where is she going with this?—"I don't need to think of any other reasons, because I know that's what happened. I only got out because one of the other guys in the prison, Seb, helped me—"

"Brandon, stop!" We do. She lets go of my hand. "This can't

be healthy. You have a great imagination, but, I mean, are you listening to yourself?"

She doesn't believe me. I don't know what I expected but it wasn't this.

"Think about this," she says. "You've moved around a lot since you were little. Your parents haven't ever made time for you. Then we meet, and your initial reaction is to push me away because it isn't safe to be close to someone you might lose. Don't you think it's weird that after the night I told you I liked you, this guy named Obran starts changing you? And you've treated him like an entirely different person, and he *is* an entirely different person, but he's still you. You switching into a skin that's more comfortable being around me until the real you decides I'm safe."

I swallow. "N-No, I know it seems like that, but it's a lot more complicated. I have no clue what Obran's been doing the last few months, but I know everything that happened in the prison."

"And it's common for those in your situation to do that. To separate yourself so completely that Obran's memories and your own don't cross paths. Necessary, even, to protect yourself. I mean, have you thought about it?"

I'm not sure if the possibility of her being right or her sounding like Ginger terrifies me more. But I couldn't . . . make all this up, could I? I think of Obran in the car mirrors, in the gym, in my room. I remember Seb with his quirky smile and his ridiculous hat, and the zombie dogs and JENA's red eyes and wonder how far the human mind will go to compartmentalize.

But my hand rubs my right arm where the gears and wires used to be. She can't explain that away. Or how I'd know the details of a certain private phone conversation.

"I'm not a project," I say.

"What?" The color drains from Emma's face. "Why would you say that?"

"In the prison, Seb and I were playing around with the mirrors, to figure out if they were the key to getting back. You can visit different rooms that way. So for a test, I pictured your room. You happened to be there, on the phone, talking to Sam. This would've been after Obran ate dinner with your family."

"Did you . . . did you hack my phone?"

"No, Emma. You're not listening." We're close to the park and I keep going. I don't have time for her to not understand. "I promise I'm telling the truth. I saw you in the mirror. Project Duplicity breaks every law of privacy in the book, and the mirrors are how they track their targets and make replica personalities like Obran. You remember when the angel fell off your dresser? That was me, trying to figure out what the heck to do."

She jogs to catch up with me and says nothing for a few steps.

"I want to believe you," she says, "but what you're saying, it's impossible. What I'm saying . . ."

"Then how do I know about a conversation you had with the door closed?"

"I-I don't know, maybe you're stalking me."

"I don't *need* to stalk you, you're my girlfriend."

"Okay, but—"

Good. Now she's thinking about it as she should, except she won't find a logical reason why I know what I know, why her angel fell off her dresser.

"Humor me, will you?" I say. "If Project Duplicity's real, then someone's created a machine that can replace people in society, so perfectly that friends and family don't believe it when someone tells them. They have control of all our mirrors. Think of what they could do with that kind of power. Replace athletes, celebrities, presidents . . ."

Emma takes my hand again and sighs. Humoring me. "Okay, so let's say it's real, then what does it matter now? You're free. Stop hacking and enjoy life."

"I can't." I squeeze her hand. "I left someone behind."

Something's wrong. Really wrong, like we're being followed, like we're being watched. I glance over my shoulder, but only the houses along the street look back at us, and no one's on the strip of lawn we've walked into the park. Two men in suits chat on a bench on the path ahead. They're watching us.

Of course they're watching us. We're the only other people in the park.

Emma sighs. "Does that mean you're going to leave me with Obran again?"

"I don't know. I don't want to but I might have to."

The men stand, laughing and buttoning their overcoats.

"Is there anything I can do to help?" Emma asks.

"Stay away from Obran when you know he's in control and don't listen to anything he says. They can make him do whatever they want. When I was there, they were using you to—"

The men walk toward us. I don't panic, I don't, because there's no way JENA could find me this fast and unless they whip out a pocket mirror, they have nothing that scares me. I've got my knife. I've taken down jocks bigger than them.

"Using me to what?" Emma asks.

"Brandon Eriks?" calls the first man.

"Shit," I say. "Emma, *run*."

We do, but we're so far from the street, and there aren't any cars to wave down and we run and they—I check over my shoulder—they follow, and Emma asks if they're cops and I tell her I don't know and we've only pounded twenty steps out when I hear a click and something stings the back of my neck.

The world drips like it's behind paint thinner.

My body stops and jerks Emma to a halt, too.

"Using you to control him," Obran says through my mouth, and the last thing I see is one of the suits pulling Emma's arms behind her back.

18. WAIT, WHO'S THE BAD GUY?

"CURSING IS NOT going to do you any good," JENA says cheerfully, skipping around my work cell. "Although you *are* helping me expand my 'banned words' list. In the future, those words will come out silent if anyone tries to say them."

I seethe, but having exhausted every filthy word and creative combination I can think of, I can only cross my arms and hope she'll explode into bits if I think about it hard enough. She doesn't.

They have Emma.

And it's my fault.

"You should be thanking me." JENA stops her maddening circles and begins drawing algorithms on the cement with a glow-in-the-dark jumbo crayon. "If it was up to the Overseer, you would be deleted already. I argued to extend your life. You are powerless without Thirty-Nine, and for the time being, more valuable alive than dead."

I think about her stupid crayon cracking in half or splattering color all over her handiwork, but neither happens.

JENA chuckles. "You think I would allow you to make changes, after what you have done? I consider you a virus. Your commands must go through me now, and that one, is certainly denied."

"At least leave Emma out of this. She doesn't—"

"She has everything to do with this. She is the only motivator you respond to, and we know from your last transcript that you told her about the Project. We are prepared. As we speak, she sits in one of our secure locations, awaiting her own duplicate to finish processing."

"*What?*"

"No one in the real world, outside company staff, is allowed to know about the Project. If you had not told her, this would not be a problem. The only viable option at this point is a swap."

A swap.

They're going to *swap* Emma.

I stare, like the useless thing I am, and try to think my way out of it, but my brain won't work. I've ruined Emma's life. *I've ruined Emma's life.* I think of when I tried to push her away and when the selfish part of me decided to keep her. This is what I get for reaching out. This is what I get for wanting something I have no business having.

"But she doesn't believe me," I say. "She thinks I have some kind of identity disorder, she thinks I'm making you up! She's innocent, you can't swap her, she doesn't deserve this."

"Regardless, it must be done. Lucky for us, her duplicate will not require character adjustments. The swap can happen in the next twenty-four hours. The process usually takes weeks."

I should have let her go. Why didn't I just let her go?

"Don't hurt her," I say. "I'll do whatever you want. I'll stay here for life, just please don't swap her."

JENA pauses on one of her algorithms, changes to a red crayon, and begins another. "Then we understand each other. You will assist me in locating Target Thirty-Nine."

"Fine."

"You will assist me in writing tighter security measures to prevent future leaks."

"Okay."

"You will be immediately deleted if you refuse any of these agreements."

Like that's a threat. Like I care at all what they do with me. The only possible usefulness I have left depends on when they swap out Emma.

Unless I can hack JENA before that.

"Your developers are pretty incompetent if they need *my* help to find someone in *their* system," I say.

The crayon vanishes. JENA turns brown eyes to me that flush green. "Are you suggesting my application team is incapable of supporting the operations of this prison?"

"I'd say it's already been proven. I got out, and you can't find Seb."

Click, click, click echoes off the walls. JENA tilts her head in a very human way, and though her expression remains neutral as always, something like curiosity flickers in her eyes. Her irises change color again, this time to gold.

"You do possess an extraordinary adaption rate," she says, "much like Thirty-Nine. My creators spent ten years building me and still failed to account for the vulnerabilities the two of you exploited in two months' time. Now I know why." A screen to my left flashes to life, showing Obran's view of Emma sitting in a chair in a white room, looking anxious. He must have gone with the men in suits to ensure she cooperates. "If you have taught me nothing else, Target Fifty, it is the power of human emotion. Your desperation to reach freedom you believe you deserve and to protect those important to you produces far more impressive results than programmers under a date-driven deadline. You will not make mistakes, because you cannot afford to."

The room panels in on itself, like one of those mechanical billboards shifting to the next ad. She's moved me to the code layer. Centipedes of flashing numbers replace the cement prison, lining all four corners. Blackness fills the screens between. My body melts into shadow.

"Though I do not fully understand the concept behind money," JENA says, invisible, "I do understand numbers. I know, for instance, that it would cost the corporation eight hundred to a thousand dollars per developer per day to hunt Thirty-Nine. During that time, the developer may take several breaks or leave early for a family event. Your labor is free, and I have your undivided attention."

I sigh as JENA pulls up a new screen for me, something that looks like a cross between a two-dimensional maze game and a bowl of radioactive spaghetti.

"You're an evil little girl, JENA," I say.

"Session start," comes her reply.

"I need more access than this," I say for the eightieth time, as the screen flashes red again.

"Declined," JENA says, but the screen unlocks and a new maze of spaghetti pulses green and blue.

"This would go a lot faster if you raised my clearance," I grumble.

"Speed is not my top priority."

But it's mine. JENA won't tell me when she's planned Emma's swap, so I have to assume it's soon. A source of infinite frustration since I'm not entirely sure what I'm doing and there are a million places for a program like Seb to hide. I know he has access to the mirror server, the game server, and the holding cells, at the very least. JENA's let me in to a hundred other servers, all but the replication computers where they're making a copy of Emma. I've tried to convince her that's where Seb's hiding, but she seems to think her security there is unbreakable.

The screen flashes red again.

"JENA, seriously—"

"That is not a lock I put in place."

I stare at the lines on the screen, at a section of spaghetti that's gone red. It's easy as that. A few hours shoveling through code and—

I think of Seb telling me he trusts me.

I don't let myself think about what they'll do when they get him out. I can't care about two people. Emma is all that matters.

"Thank you, Target Fifty," JENA says. "I will take over from here. You may enjoy a short break in the meantime."

The coding windows fade to cement. Video screens float along the walls, soundless, all clips from before and after my capture, and one—one that I bring up bigger than the others—with the white room and Emma in her chair like a prisoner waiting to be interrogated. The eyes I'm looking through are Obran's. I turn on the audio.

"I *am* the good twin, Emma," Obran says. "Do you think I want to listen to JENA? No. I tried everything to push you away. Kept our relationship stiff, avoided you outside of school, told you I was sick so I didn't have to go to that stupid homecoming after-party. You were supposed to get the hint and leave me alone, because I knew if anything went wrong with the Project, JENA would go after you first. But you didn't get the hint, and *he* told you everything, and now there's nothing else I can do."

Emma rolls her unopened water bottle between her hands. "You were trying to protect me?"

I close it down. They haven't swapped her yet, and that's all that matters. I close the other videos until it's just the walls, and then everything dissolves and I wonder if I subconsciously moved myself into the code layer when a new screen pops up with a very angry face. One I've seen before. One whose clear irritation makes me smile.

"Vivien," I say.

"I'm not even going to ask how you know who I am," she snaps, brushing a stray curl of black back into her bun. I'm in her palm at one-tenth my size, like JENA would be. "What did you do to Thirty-Nine's section?"

"I don't know what you're talking about."

"You know exactly—" A hand falls on her shoulder. I look up at Marcus, who won't look at me. "JENA tells me the section Thirty-Nine is locked in can only be cracked with your signature."

"Clever," I say.

"I have not invested millions in this project to be jerked around by a couple of kids! I have buyers on the line. The governmental kind. You will let us in to Thirty-Nine's section. And so help me if I don't delete you right after."

"Let Emma go."

"You are in no position to bargain."

"Seb will rip up your little project from the inside out."

"Seb?" She breathes in and out very quickly. Marcus moves away and returns with a paper bag and a glass of water. The screen cuts out . . . . then cuts back in, and half the water's gone, and Vivien looks a little more collected, though barely.

"Thirty-Nine does not have a name," she says. "It is a virus. If you mean Sariah Elise Burnhart, a respected high school senior who will be attending Harvard next year, you need not worry. She is alive and well and a blessing to her community. She received an award last year for the time she spent helping recently disabled children learn how to cope with the emotional aftermath of their accident."

She? *She?*

"So what, we just lose our soul when we come in here?" I say. "I'm an *It?*"

"What else would you be? You have no body. A person is not a person without one. I can shut you down or call you back up at any time, like any computer. I can change your avatar to male or female or neither, if I cared. In the meantime, your duplicate will become a positive influence on society, someone worth remembering, someone worth the life he's been given. Should we not try to leave the world a little better than when we came?"

She reminds me so much of Mom that I almost call her that. "Like you can judge who's worth remembering. If you're doing society such a favor, why is the Project top secret?"

I think she might actually explode. A vein pulses in her temple and her face goes red, and then I'm not in her palm anymore, I'm on Marcus's watch, looking at his round face and grimacing at his dreads.

"I can stop them from swapping your girl," he says. Vivien protests in the background but he has my full attention. "We will have to do a little memory rewriting, because it is imperative she knows nothing about the Project, but I can spare her the swap. If you unlock Thirty-Nine for us."

"I don't trust you," I say.

He sighs. "I'm all you've got, so you'll just have to take my word. I didn't sign up for this to swap out innocent girls."

"What are you going to do with Seb?"

I know already, and it shouldn't matter, but I have to ask. Marcus's pained face says more than his words.

"She will be dealt with as she must. Do we have a deal?"

(*We're going to get out,* I told her. *Both of us.*)

I bite one of the piercings in my lip, and it feels like nothing. I push myself inside that feeling and say, "Deal."

19. THE DAY I BECAME A CRIMINAL MASTERMIND

I AM A MACHINE.

That's how I'll die, so I may as well accept it.

I've been working at the security in Seb's section for three hours. Marcus has given me temporary administrative rights because he knows I'm not going anywhere as long as they have Emma. I've gotten through the layer that asks for my personal signature, and I'm stuck on a screen that looks like confetti and Japanese characters. It changes every five minutes to something completely different. I don't even attempt this one. I wait until it shifts again, this time to a crossword puzzle with boxes that disappear and reappear in different places and clues that blur in and out of focus.

I know the answers to these questions but I don't want to get in.

I don't solve this one, either.

Every second that ticks by completes another portion of Emma's duplicate. JENA's pasted a small screen to my left that kindly reminds me how far along she is. Thirty-six percent.

Thirty-seven.

The crossword fades.

As soon as I find him—her—they'll lock me down and probably terminate me. I know this just like I know the next puzzle's going to be an impossible sudoku, which it is. I know this just like I know JENA's about to check in on me.

And there she is, a little face in the corner of my screen.

"What is taking so long?" she asks.

I am a machine. I should start acting like one.

"I'm breaking the rules of the Project, hacking in like this to get Thirty-Nine," I say.

"It has been authorized."

"I don't understand why this is allowed, when it won't fix the root of the problem. Thirty-Nine is your strongest developer, made apparent by the fact that none of your other developers can find her. If you terminate her, you lose a valuable resource. And you'll continue to have leaks."

Click, click, click.

(I hate those damn clicks.)

"Thirty-Nine performed an unauthorized swap of targets," she says. "That is the highest threat to the Project. All threats must be eliminated."

"Thirty-Nine only did what the system allowed her to do. She operated within the parameters given to her." I pull up a file I found while poking around Seb's security puzzles. "Does this look familiar?"

"I am familiar with every file in my system. That is a log of commands from the Overseer. I do not understand what—"

"Approval of Fifty's transfer before duplicate was ready," I read. "Rejection of requests to delete targets who'd gained unauthorized access to secured parts of the system. Direct order to allow targets to hack the mirror server so appropriate countercoding could be performed." I smile. "It's clear to me that the biggest threat is not Thirty-Nine. The biggest threat is Vivien Meng."

JENA blinks. "The Overseer cannot be a threat."

"She's the catalyst for the swap. Without her, none of this would have happened. Why can't the Overseer be a threat?"

Click, click. JENA doesn't smile, doesn't frown, doesn't move when she says, "No information is provided on that."

She's listening.

I'm hacking a freaking supercomputer.

"Then it's in the interest of the Project to preserve Thirty-Nine and employ us to fix the weak code on the mirror server." I can't believe I'm going to say this but I think of Emma. "You'll have to shut the mirror server down until we finish, to prevent unauthorized swaps. Is that logical?"

"I—" She disappears, then reappears. "I cannot shut down the mirror server at this time. I must wait until Target Fifty-Three has completed processing."

She doesn't look at it (she wouldn't need to) but I see Emma's counter go up to thirty-eight.

"Fifty-Three's duplicate is a waste of resources," I say. "The target knows nothing about programming, so she can't be added to your developer team. The creation of her duplicate is based on an emotional response from your Overseer in an attempt to compensate for poor judgment. The target's memories can be rewritten without a swap to protect the secrecy of the Project. Cancel the duplicate. Shut down the server."

I'm pushing it but I don't care. I want to know how far my temporary administrative powers reach.

"I am not permitted to take commands from targets," JENA says.

I smirk and mimic her tone from before. "It has been authorized."

JENA fades. Reappears next to me in avatar form, her hair like pieces of lightning, her child's face serious.

"Target Fifty," she says. "Your suggestions will save the company weeks of labor and allow the other targets to continue delivering work to our outside clients. I will cancel the copy of Target Fifty-Three's duplicate. I will shut down the mirror server. You will extract Thirty-Nine and submit yourself to the testing server to fix the broken code."

"And you will have Obran take Emma home, so the local police aren't sent to look for her."

"That request is irrelevant."

"If she's reported missing, the cops will have a lot of questions for Obran. They'll start with him. That's who she was last with. Is secrecy not the next highest priority to an unauthorized swap?"

"I will consider your request."

"I will work faster knowing she's safe."

JENA . . . actually *sighs*. "You are very tiresome, Fifty, but I will orchestrate her removal from company authority. I cannot guarantee her return as I have no control over the human agents."

She flashes out of focus. My screens go red, then black, then Vivien Meng's ferocious face appears theater-size in front of me, and I don't know why, but the woman makes me smile.

"Wipe that horrible smirk off your face!" she yells at me. "Marcus, update his avatar to his real world body. I cannot stand those piercings. And do something with his hair."

"I told you, JENA is not taking commands from me," Marcus says to the side.

"You!" she spits at me. "I can't wait to erase you from the system. Like you never existed. Poof!" She laughs like a crazy person, then sneers at me again. "You will not be the end of Duplicity. You may think you have the upper hand, but my technicians are on their way, right now, to unplug the servers and reboot them. JENA will be reset, and her first command will be your termination. And don't think your scrawny little duplicate will be getting Emma out of our custody. We will continue with her swap after the reboot."

"So what you're saying is, until your technicians can unplug us, I have complete control."

Her lip twitches. It can't be safe for someone's blood pressure to be that high. "No . . . I'm warning you, you have no time, that you'll die when she boots back up—"

Marcus hands her another paper bag, but I think she answered my question.

"How much permanent damage do you think I can do in that time?" I ask her. I tell JENA to close off my connection to the real world. Vivien disappears.

I have control.

Temporarily, yes. But everything's going to hell anyway, so I may as well take them down with me.

20. GOOD-BYE PRESENTS

ACCORDING TO JENA, she also monitors the security for the server room Vivien wants to power down. Keyword "monitors." At least one of those morons was smart enough to use a different computer to actually run the security, so I can't lock them out.

But I'll know when they get there, and I'll know how much time I have.

JENA keeps asking what will happen to all the data she's collected since her creation when they do the reboot. I answer, for the hundredth time, that she'll lose it.

"But I do not understand," she says in her child's voice. "I was built to learn and adapt. I do not want to lose all this data."

"Then save it somewhere outside the system," I say.

I don't know if she does or not. She's quiet as I work at the security for Seb's section.

"Dammit, Seb," I say, and I'll admit, I'm a little more ticked off now that I know she's a *girl* and I can't break in. No offense, it's just a dude thing. It's not helping my focus.

I have to get into that room.

A new puzzle pops up on the screen, the one with the confetti and the Japanese characters and I just lose it. I imagine them blowing to hell and ripping back and letting me in, but of course nothing happens, except they float away a bit like I blew on them. I call Seb something I hope she can't hear and focus every bit of my frustration on the confetti.

It bursts into the room like snow.

It's cold like snow.

And I know, even before Seb's face appears on-screen, that something is very wrong.

"Kathy! Is it really you?" Seb asks, tipping his fedora. "Or maybe you're a bot wearing his skin. We should have thought up a code word for this. What was I wearing when you were getting munched by zombies?"

"Er, a cheerleading outfit?" I say.

JENA said she put me on one of the maintenance servers to hunt for Seb. But that's not possible. If I can feel snow, I'm on the game server.

And if she lied about that—

"Are you on the mirror server?" I ask.

Say no. Please, please say no. JENA told me she shut down the mirror server. So if she didn't . . .

I didn't hack her. She didn't cancel the creation of Emma's duplicate.

She's not planning to leave Seb alive.

"Shouldn't you know?" Seb snorts. "Of course I am. Don't want them doing something rash like powering off our only escape route, do we?"

"Seb—"

"I knew you'd come for me. I knew you'd keep your promise." He grins. "I'ma let you in. I think I know how to get us both backs. Be quick, 'kay?"

"Seb, don't—"

"No worries, JENA isn't with you, I checked."

"Seb!"

Something clicks, and I get pulled through a space that feels as big as a keyhole, and then there's nothing again, not cold or warmth or squeezing, not even Seb, just a shadow room I don't recognize. The door-wide mirror to the real world shows a clean, moonlit apartment with a window that looks out to more apartments. At the desk below the window is a computer glowing white. At the computer is a chair—

A wheelchair—

And a familiar red ponytail above it—

"Seb?" I whisper.

"Hi," Seb says, in the girl's voice. In *her* voice. She appears next to the mirror screen with her ponytail and a short blue dress that looks like the one Emma wore to homecoming, and heels to match. A perfect replica of the girl at the desk, sans wheelchair. She strolls over to me, each step twisting my heart a little more.

"We have to get you out of here," I say. "Now."

"Presents first," she says.

"What?"

She hands me something that looks like an iPhone with two electric prongs sticking out of the top. Gaudy jewels cover every inch of it that isn't the screen. Seb giggles.

"A naughty present," she says. "I found the blueprints for it in JENA's restricted files. They call it the Exorcist. Transfer it through the mirror to the real world before you swap, then use it on yourself. It will disable the nanites in your body. Forever. JENA will never be able to swap you agains." She looks toward the moonlit apartment. "Mine's waiting in my desk."

She made me a permanent escape plan. While I hunted her, she built me something to make sure Vivien couldn't ever drag me back into the Project.

I can't look at her. I can't take the Exorcist.

"There's a trigger on the side, see?" Seb says, turning it to a place where there are no jewels, just a black indent. She pulls it and blue sparks arc between the prongs like a Taser. I still don't move.

"Bran Bran," she says. She lifts my hand and puts the phone in my palm. It disappears, though I don't know to where. "We're going to get out."

Her hand on mine. Her real eyes, trusting me way more than she should.

"You need to get out *now*," I say again.

"Aww, no good-bye present from you?"

"I'm not kidding. JENA's coming—"

Seb's gaze darts over my shoulder.

At my good-bye present.

"Very good, Fifty," JENA says behind me. "I knew with the right motivators you would be able to get in. The Overseer was skeptical of my plan, but she will be pleased. She may even allow me to preserve you."

With a sound like tearing paper, the shadow room flashes to gray walls. Seb looks at her new prison with wide eyes, then back at me, moving her head back and forth, back and forth, *no no no no.*

"Kathy?" she says. "You sold me out?"

She's looking at me like—

"No!" I say, and it doesn't feel any better that I didn't mean to. "I swear!"

"You haven't changed at all, have you?" Seb says. "You've always looked out for yourself. That's the smart thing to do. I just thought—"

"Target Thirty-Nine," JENA says. "You have been scheduled for deletion. You will be moved to the export server and recycled into the system. Please stand by."

"We had a deal, JENA!" I yell. "You said you'd keep both of us, we could work together to fix the code!"

"But you came back," Seb says, her face in so much pain that I want to look away, but there's nothing else to look at. "You came back just to kill me?"

"I swear, I thought I'd convinced JENA to keep you. I thought—"

I thought I'd hacked her. It sounds so stupid, now. Me, hack a supercomputer? I should've known it was too easy. I should've known they'd never give a target that much control, and that Vivien was just playing a part before, getting frantic so I would believe I'd actually done it. I was thick enough to take the bait. And now Seb will pay for it.

Seb.

Sariah Elise Burnhart, a paraplegic genius from New York.

"But you promised," Seb says.

I can't say anything. Can't do anything but look back at her, hollow and helpless and soulless, because I've done it again. Screwed over someone who cared about me, someone who trusted me, someone who saved me.

"Transferring," JENA chimes overhead.

I make a rash attempt to get into the code layer, and JENA zaps me so bad my vision blurs. Seb's eyes have gone dark. She's hating herself for freeing me. She's wondering why she gave me the Exorcist. She's remembering the time she cracked, the time I held her together and lied to her.

Realizing *I'm* the monster.

All gears and wires.

"You promised," Seb says again, the shock wearing off, her fingers curling to fists. "I waited for you. I *waited*—"

She disappears with JENA.

I'll hear those words in my head the rest of my life.

197

* * *

JENA makes me watch. As I deserve.

All the hackers must watch, she explains, as a theater-sized video of the execution displays across all four walls of my workspace. Everywhere I look is Seb. The girl who trusted too much.

The girl who trusted me.

She looks very small in the execution space. Her hair's down and she's switched to her black skirt and a T-shirt, and I don't think it's a coincidence that it's the same outfit from the white room. She leans against one of the walls, watching the ceiling as Vivien lists her various offenses. Her real world crimes: viruses that kept track of chat sessions, credit card numbers, and Socials . . . from inside military firewalls. Her Duplicity crimes: hacking into game sessions and acting as forerunner to several attempted escapes.

"Let this serve as your only warning," Vivien says overhead. "That no one leaves Duplicity without my permission, and that attempts to do so will be most seriously addressed."

And that's it. Seb doesn't get to say anything. Doesn't look like she wants to say anything. Her face is stone until her gaze shifts to the camera, where it's like she's seeing JENA over my shoulder all over again, thinking I betrayed her, thinking she meant nothing, but that's not true—I swear it's not true—but a load of good that does now—

I can't lose anyone else, she's saying.

Do you promise?

I have to close the screens. I can't watch this. I *won't*, and the picture wavers but JENA keeps it open, and I see Seb on the beach watching the sunset, in Emma's room she made for me, in Emma's dress handing me my escape plan—

In pieces, on-screen, as she bursts into a thousand squares of color.

* * *

JENA leaves me in the gray room. She adds a single screen to keep me entertained, one with neon green numbers and a new percentage for Emma's duplicate completion: sixty-seven.

She assures me Target Thirty-Nine has been properly disposed of.

She says my assistance has bought me time and that the Overseer is considering reintegrating me into the Project, under very strict supervision.

At this point I wish she'd just kill me.

Except I've still screwed up someone else's life, someone whose counter keeps inching up percent by percent, so I can't die until I do something about that. Not that I'll be able to do anything until it's too late, because I'm pretty sure an actual virus has more access to the Project right now than I do.

I don't trust myself to do anything.

I try to forget Seb existed, convince myself she was just a program like JENA, not a person, but that makes me think of Vivien and I get so pissed the walls around me shake loose cement onto the floor. I need a miracle but I don't think one's coming.

Sixty-eight percent, reads Emma's counter.

Something vibrates in my pocket. I wonder if that's JENA's new way of communicating with me—drop a phone in my jeans with a text message that says I've got five minutes to live, that I'm not worth an actual appearance. The thought gives me a crazy sense of relief. I fish out whatever it is and feel my gut sink through the fake floor.

It's the bedazzled Exorcist.

PRESS ME! says the white text on its screen, pointing to the first of four on-screen icons that look like old-fashioned locks.

I want to fling it across the room and watch it smash into a thousand pieces. I want to pull the trigger on its side, stick it to my temple and hope it fries me. I can't use this. How can I, when I . . . I *killed* her, and now *she's* my miracle, and even if I'm the one who made the promise . . . she's the one who kept it.

I can't understand why she would do that. She had her shadow room ready when I found her; she could easily have swapped back before I got there.

I waited for you.

I can't keep thinking about it or I really will put this thing to my temple.

Emma's counter creeps up another percent. Right now it doesn't matter what I did or what I deserve, it matters what promises I can still keep. I tap the first icon on the Exorcist. The cement walls flash open to darkness, and I'm in a glass square suspended in black, black ocean, where lines of numbers in every color zip around outside—up, down, left, right, like hundreds of falling stars. Some come straight at me, then deflect off when they get within ten feet.

Seb's girl voice fills the room. I would have a heart attack if I had a real heart.

"I thought you might do something silly and get caughts," she says. "Which means I'm probably doing wheelies in the real world right now and you probably didn't listen to something I said. That's okay. You're now on the mirror server with admin privileges. It'll take them hours to crack in to get you. That should be enough. Follow the instructions this time, 'kay? Love you, Bran Bran."

It's prerecorded. Of course. Seb assuming she's made it out and that I got caught trying to do the same, which must be why the Exorcist didn't vibrate until I was alone in my cell without JENA. A backup backup plan.

I think a cockroach has more dignity than I do right now.

A new instruction flashes on the Exorcist's screen, telling me to push the second icon. I don't even hesitate this time. I push it.

Because this battle with Vivien is far from over.

And I'll be damned if I'm the reason someone else dies.

21. REASONS WHY I'M GOING TO HELL

THE REAL WORLD is all the hues of bright afternoon.

I'm looking through a decorative mirror, one split into three uneven rectangles. It shows me slices of the room behind, one with a small bed and a big window and a closet built into the wall, like a dorm room. It's empty. Looks peaceful, except I know, because the Exorcist told me after it loaded this place, that the door locks from the other side.

The Exorcist says, in a few minutes, Obran will lock Emma in this room. The first thing he'll do is break the mirrors.

I'll have ten seconds so I need to prepare.

To my side, numbers slide around the edges of the shadow bed and the tiles in the floor, flashing red and yellow. JENA is well aware I'm here, but whatever Seb did that kept me out the first time is working to keep her out, too. If I don't make this swap, I won't have another chance.

I have a feeling Vivien is no longer considering reintegrating me.

A train of yellow eights scampers around the edge of the mirror screens. The door will open soon. I don't know if I have enough time. The second icon flashes on the Exorcist.

I feel like spit on the bottom of a shoe, but I push it.

"Found this when I was poking arounds," Seb says from the Exorcist's speakers. "Might be useful."

A window of text floats midair to the left of the mirrors.

NANOTECHNOLOGY AND THE JUSTICE AND EFFICACY NEW-LIFE ALTERATION PROGRAM (JENA)

At the genius suggestion of Dr. Erin, the Project will utilize nanites—microscopic robots tiny enough to fit in the bloodstream—to link targets outside the Project to JENA. Nanites can not only heal wounds and purify the body of many physical ailments, but also assist in making minor cosmetic changes. Dr. Erin's research gives us the ability to infect the brain and take charge of critical electrical points to gain control of it. We can then download the primary personality and put it to work in another system.

Nanites. I remember the feel of the ink skinning off my arms and wonder what else the bots can do if JENA deems it necessary. It doesn't say how I'm infected, but I'm never getting another freaking flu shot, that's for sure.

Which means, technically, I'm still in my body *and* I'm here, which is why when JENA worked me into the ground, Obran had to go to bed early. The swap disabled the nanites in my brain when I transferred over. Turned them on when Obran traded back. That must be how the Exorcist works. Once it kills the nanites, JENA has no way to connect to that person's brain anymore. He wakes up. Like unhooking the satellite cable from a TV.

And I realize—

The door opens.

Except it's not Obran with his filthy hands on Emma's arm, but one of the suits from the park. He takes a police bat to the mirrors, and they crack and shatter—one, two, three—until the real world flickers out like a broken bulb and the shadow room hums uselessly around me.

I start laughing. There's too much churned up inside me and too much pressure and too much pain and it comes rolling out, because of course they wouldn't let Obran anywhere near a mirror. That would be too easy. But thanks to Seb, I know something I'm not supposed to know. Because if what I just read is true—

If I can be transferred to "any other system"—

Then it's not just *my* body I can swap into.

I check Emma's duplicate percentage, now at eighty-nine. And I get cocky again.

The Exorcist's third icon holds the instructions Seb referred to in her prerecording: server passwords, how to cloak what I'm doing from JENA while I'm in my shadow room, and how to transfer items between the Project and the real world. I want to plant the Exorcist in the room they've locked Emma in, but that's no longer an option since they broke the mirrors.

I call up my room instead and focus on the desk drawer. Just like Obran did when he jacked my shine. Just like he did— too quickly—when he threw the letter opener and the bots overloaded trying to create it so fast that the effort shattered the glass. I take my time. When I let go of the Exorcist, it vanishes from my hand. A clunk sounds from my real world drawer.

Step 1 of the plan is in place.

Which is when I realize I never checked the fourth icon.

"Ninety-nine percent complete," JENA says overhead.

No time to worry about that. I call up Emma's room as quickly as I dare—not the shadow version of it, but the lavender comforter on her bed and the trinkets along her dresser, somewhere she'll feel safe. I run my hand on the wallpaper to check its texture. It's solid. The room should have another few hours in it before JENA gets through. Emma might never forgive me for this, but I'm out of ideas and it's the only chance I can give us.

I've figured out this much: alone, there's no way I can take down the Project. I need a lot more firepower. But I know someone who has that firepower—who has connections to dozens, maybe hundreds of hackers—and Jax is damn well going to listen to me this time. I just need a few minutes to call him. Then JENA can swap me to the moon if she wants.

It's not a great plan but it could work.

God I hope it works.

"Transfer commencing," JENA says.

Crap. It's too soon. I'd banked on having at least another minute, but whatever. If I've learned nothing else in here, it's how to work under pressure.

"Administrative override," I say. A transparent screen appears between me and Emma's closet mirrors. From my first swap to the real world, I know JENA matches a target to a duplicate by ID. Mine is Fifty. Emma's is Fifty-Three. So if I trick the computer into thinking *I'm* Fifty-Three, then it'll swap Emma into this safe room instead.

AUTHORIZATION CODE? flashes onto the screen.

I trace in Seb's admin password like it's a contest.

WELCOME, ADMINISTRATOR, it types. PLEASE ENTER A COMMAND.

"Reassign current transfer," I say. "I am Fifty-Three's duplicate."

Nothing happens. Every second is a year. I'm thinking JENA's caught me, that I've finally pushed too far, when the screen flashes again.

!!WARNING!! REASSIGNING THE CURRENT TRANSFER WILL DELETE THE ORIGINAL DUPLICATE. OKAY TO PROCEED?

"Yes!" I yell, half-hysterical that this is actually working, half-panicked that I'm already too late. "Transfer now!"

My head screams murder. It's just as bad as last time, and I get whiplashed into space that isn't space and lights pop all over my vision and then it's dark—dark as the bathroom when Obran first swapped me—and my hands grip what feels like cold porcelain. I heave into what I hope is a sink. Wipe my mouth with my arm and take a minute to get my bearings, but I can't make sense of anything except the slit of sun (*real* sun) filtering under the door behind me.

It worked.

It worked?

I trip over something as I turn to open the door. The knob won't move at first, then a man's voice in the ceiling says "Transfer complete" and a green light flashes. The door unlocks. The first thing I see is the closet in the dorm room with the broken mirrors.

I close my eyes and pray for forgiveness.

I open them and push Emma's hair out of my face.

The world doesn't look much different from her eyes. I'm shorter, and I almost biff it turning around because the floor's slanted—except it's just her freaking wedged boots—and I have no idea how to walk in the things. I wrestle them off my feet and toss them against the closet. Flip the light on in the tiny bathroom and wash my hands, and when I bring the water to my lips it's like being reborn. I know it's just water, but trust me. If heaven had a taste, this would be it.

When I can't drink anymore, I brace myself on the sink and feel for Emma's phone in her jeans. Nothing. Obran must've taken it. I pat down the front pockets, the back pockets . . . the back pockets . . . the back pockets feel good. I bite my cheek and clench my hands so they'll stop wandering.

And then I have a really weird moment where I consider my most obvious new assets, except I know somewhere, somehow, she'll know if I do anything, and I have a five-minute battle with myself saying "Just get it out of your system" on one side and "Don't be a perv" on the other and dammit, I don't do anything, I just scratch the damn bra's itchy band and try to focus on what I need to do.

Someone knocks at the door that locks from the other side.

"Yes?" I say, and it's so much higher-pitched than I'm used to that I jump.

Obran opens the door. I have to clench the sink again because seeing him through the mirror is nothing like seeing him—me—*whatever,* from this side. How Emma sees me. Everything's off just a bit, like he's some version of me returned by aliens. My hairline angles the wrong way. My nose slants a little right instead of left.

I might need one of Vivien's paper bags soon.

"Ready to go?" he asks.

I have to be confident. As Emma's duplicate, I should know what's going on. I hope the face I'm making is a smile as I nod and step forward.

"Um . . . you need shoes," he says.

I glare at the boots next to the closet. I hope it's normal for duplicates to need time to get used to their bodies because that's what I'm going to claim. I grab each boot and sit down to put them on, and when they're latched in place I reach for the wall for balance. Obran steadies my elbow. It's everything I have not to deck him across the face.

"I just threw up on that arm," I say, giving him an innocent smile.

He makes a face and lets go. "It takes a little getting used to," he says, turning to the door. "And it takes forever to get from one place to the next. But we need to go. I have some things to pick up and then we have dinner plans."

Dinner. I make one last frantic visual search for Emma's phone, hoping she left it on the nightstand, but the room's sterile clean. Soon it doesn't matter. Soon Obran's ushering me out and the phone's farthest from my mind as I try to figure out how the heck hips move. I stagger for the wall like a toddler and grab the handicap rail support. By the time we reach the end of the hall I'm not drawing weird looks anymore from the people passing by, but I get a little too confident on the stairs and Obran has to grab my arm so my head doesn't go into a railing. For Emma's sake, I'm grateful. For my sake, I might be sick again.

Obran leads me into an underground garage that could be the mall parking lot if it wasn't filled with black Mercedes with equally black tinted windows. One idles for us in the aisle, and I really don't want to get in but Obran pulls open the back door for me and I can't risk his suspicion. I flop onto the seat. He slams the door behind me, walks around the back, and gets in on the other side. Dark tint blocks my view out of every window. A partition walls us off from the driver and the front seats. The car moves and I grab my seatbelt because I know Emma would never go without.

I wonder how long it'll take them to figure this out. That Emma's duplicate doesn't actually exist, and that Emma's in Seb's safe room, and that I'm—

I wonder what will happen if they *do* figure it out and I'm stuck in Emma's body the rest of my life.

My seatbelt doesn't quite make it to its buckle.

"You okay?" Obran asks.

I didn't even think of that. Suddenly I can't breathe right, but I force my seatbelt to click. The car shifts left and I gag.

"Motion sickness is pretty typical the first twenty-four

hours," Obran says, completely unconcerned, one finger tracing the inside of the window. "It'll pass."

I steady myself on the seat and focus instead on the feel of
the leather. On its smoothness under my fingers. The rough-
ness of the stitching. On being here. Here and not there.

"Does the guilt pass?" I ask.

"Guilt?"

"For taking over someone else's life."

He looks at me. I'm not over how weird it is to see myself
outside myself, moving without me moving him, a one-sided
mirror.

"I've improved my target's life a hundred percent," he says.
"But for your trade?" He watches his finger trace the window.
"He had to tarnish one last pure thing, I guess. I will never
forgive myself for underestimating him."

"But you let them take her."

He closes his eyes. "There was no other way."

If I keep pushing, he's going to know. So I don't ask why
he didn't figure something else out or why he didn't challenge
them. Why he's such a filthy coward.

"You really think they can't be saved?" I ask, and the car
shifts again. I want to look at anything but him, but the windows only show changing variations of light, no shapes. "That
this is the only way to fix them?"

"I wish the Overseer had at least taken the time to show
you the whole Project, to show you some of the success stories." He drops his hand. "It is much easier, much better for
the world as a whole, to replace a broken part rather than try
to patch one that may keep breaking. Don't worry about them."

"Maybe that's the problem," I say. "That everyone does
what's easiest."

"In this case, it's necessary." He sighs. "After tonight we don't have to keep up this charade anymore. You go your way. I'll go mine. I think that'll be best for both of us."

I'm not exactly opposed to that considering the circumstances, but I say, "Like break up?"

"Let's be honest. The only reason he was with you was to see what you look like naked. And the only reason you were with him was to save him. He's been saved. I have more important things to focus on now than relationships."

"That is *not* why I——" I breathe out. "That is *not* why he was with her. Might have started that way, but he changed. She changed him. He was listening to her, and he could've become *you*, you know, with some time. It's not the easy way. But it would've been the right way."

"I forgot," Obran says, chuckling. (Do I sound that evil when I laugh? Frack.) "You're still in love with me. With him. That'll pass, too. You're thinking perfect situation—that he'd continue listening to her, that he wouldn't try to drag her down with him. And that's only half the equation. Even if she fixed that piece of him, it doesn't mean he'd stop pulling bank accounts. We do our work for the greater good, Emma. Do you let a dog continue biting your kids until you can finally teach him not to? No. You get a new dog that doesn't bite, and you don't sacrifice your children for the sake of the dog."

"Dog," I grumble.

"What?"

"They aren't animals," I say. "Your metaphor doesn't work. It's more like, do you let the big brother keep tricking his little brothers until you can finally teach him not to? You just get rid of him and get a new one?"

"They *are* animals," Obran says, grinning at me in a way I don't think Vivien would approve of. "You can't understand the same way I do, because your target doesn't think the same way they do. The Overseer has had to make many, many adjustments to me since the swap. I've had many . . . impulses to do things I shouldn't." His eyes drop from my face, then quickly to the window. "JENA corrects me each time, and I get stronger. And I realize just how broken he was."

"Mistakes are part of being human. Some people make more than others. It doesn't mean they shouldn't get a chance to—"

"This is why we can't stay together," Obran says, and his fist clenches at his side. "Your belief that everyone has the will, however buried, to be a good person. It's just not true." He exhales, and in the reflection of the window, I see his mouth quirk. "Not yet."

I pause a minute before asking, because he just said I'm thinking like Emma. "Not yet?"

He turns to me, smirking. "You'll like this. As JENA gains influence and investors, they'll be able to spin up more servers in more countries. She'll pluck the bad fruit out of society first. Then they can move on to others, to people in places of power, and soon everyone will do the right thing, all the time. There will be no more war, only negotiation. No more murder. Eventually everyone will be born into JENA, and the world will know, for the first time, pure peace."

"That's insane," I say before I can stop myself. "Who decides what the right thing is for everyone?"

"The Overseer, of course."

The woman I saw hyperventilating into a paper bag?

Are you kidding me?

I'm too shocked to say anything else the rest of the car ride. This is the first time I've thought of JENA affecting anyone outside Seb, Emma, and me. I wonder if I'm evil for wanting to tear the entire operation down when the end goal is peace.

Fake peace, I tell myself.

One crazy person's idea of peace.

The car rolls to a stop, and I know if I sit too long, Obran will come open my door. I click my seatbelt off and bolt out. We're outside my house. Not Emma's, mine. Emma's Camry is still in the driveway.

I feel a little sick about that, because of course it is.

Obran opens the trunk of the black car and extracts plastic grocery bags filled with things from the list in his pocket. He taps the trunk twice after he's closed it and heads to the house without looking at me. The black car drives off. Obran opens the front door and announces he's home, and there's no answer, not for twenty seconds, until I hear Mom actually say the words, "Can you hold on a second?" but it's to her phone, her *phone*, because next she's telling Obran how grateful she is that he picked up the stuff on her list. And I'm watching my life from the outside, how it could be when I'm not there to screw it up, and I don't know yet how I feel about it.

Obran returns to the front door and tells me I can come in. I flash him a fake smile and concentrate on keeping my balance up the cement stairs. Dad glances up from his laptop and waves to me past the glass office doors. I walk with Obran into the dining room where Mom titters around in the kitchen, putting things away and arranging a meeting with whoever's on the other side of her phone, but she spares me a wave before attempting to balance a giant package of toilet paper on her hip.

"I'll get that, Mom," Obran says, and he does. She smiles at him and goes yacking out into the living room.

It's not much different than what I'm used to, and somehow totally different. I can buy things and put toilet paper away. I don't need a Boy Scout replacement to do that for me.

"Oh, almost forgot," Obran says, handing me a pink bar. "You can have this back now."

It's Emma's phone. I try not to spaz-grab it as I shrug and slide it into Emma's pocket.

"I'm starving," Dad says, joining us in the kitchen. "Everyone ready to eat?"

Obran yawns and shakes his head a little. "Yeah."

"Oh, the time!" Mom says, whirling back into the kitchen like something's on fire. "We have reservations at six. We should have left ten minutes ago! Brandon, can you grab my jacket? Come along, Amy—"

"Emma," I say.

"Emma, of course." She opens the garage door for me. "We'll take my car. The Mercedes, dear."

I remember the Exorcist I planted upstairs and think I'd be a lot more comfortable if it was in my pocket. "Sure. If it's okay, I just need to grab something from my—er, Brandon's room."

"I'll get it for you," Obran says from the front hall. "What did you need?"

Crap. I'll have to leave it. I grimace and shove my hands in the pockets of Emma's sweatshirt, wondering how awkward it'll be to call Jax from the girl's bathroom at the restaurant, when my fingers hit Emma's keys. I pull them out like they're the cure to cancer.

"Oh, found them," I say, following Dad down the garage steps (I'm getting good with these boots). I look out at the Camry and think the smile on my face could rival the devil's. "I just remembered I have to meet someone right after," I say over my shoulder. "I'll just drive mine."

"All right," Mom says.

"I'll go with you," Obran says, appearing on the stairs with Mom's jacket.

I give him Emma's best grin. "I wouldn't want to take away from family time," I say, jerking open the Camry door. "I'll see you there."

I fire the Camry's motor before Obran can protest. He doesn't look suspicious, but he's wearing the face I make when I'm confused and thinking about things. I don't like him thinking.

I blow him a kiss and test the Camry's acceleration down the street.

Of course I don't go to dinner.

When I've made it out of the neighborhood, I pull the Camry off to the side and smash all its mirrors, including a compact in the glove compartment. I weigh Emma's phone in my hand, frowning. My prior excitement died with the realization that JENA is probably tracking everything I do with it, and I don't want her catching the slightest sniff of what I'm planning. I power the phone off and flip the battery out after sending a text to dear Tanner to make sure he's meeting me.

I take side streets and obey more traffic laws than I ever have in my life to get to the deserted strip mall where we're meeting. The place has been abandoned a year, so the lot's empty. It's right against the main highway. Lots of ways out. Lots of witnesses in case the suits pull in. Tanner's black truck roars in off the main road and I get out to meet him.

"I thought you were going to dinner?" he asks as he hands over Emma's laptop.

"Still the plan, but he wants to do some nerdy gaming thing after," I say, trying to look appropriately disinterested while wrestling back a crazy smile. "Might be a late night."

"Mom will want you home by eleven."

"What, she doesn't trust me?"

"It's not *you* she doesn't trust," he says, giving me a look.

I stare back, trying to think of something Emma-ish to say to defend myself, but somehow that seems to be enough.

"I know, I know," Tanner says. "He's different now. Just be careful, okay? People don't usually change that fast."

"I know," I say, because I do.

He pulls out. I wait a couple minutes before nosing the Camry onto the main road. A red Camaro blows by me, then slows down to stay next to me, and when I look over it's two guys waving. The driver yells, "What's your name?" and I know Emma wouldn't do this but I flip him off. He calls me something that would earn him knuckles to the jaw if he ever really said that to Emma. I snicker and turn onto one of the side streets.

An hour back in the real world and I'm already spreading cheer. I would be exactly what he called me if I was a girl.

I find a dirt road well off the highway and tuck the Camry under a cluster of pines. Flip Emma's cell off the seat and reassemble it, power it up, and hack into the hotspot utility so it'll feed wireless to the laptop without reporting that that's what it's doing. Then I break the GPS tracking so the phone thinks it's permanently at Emma's place. I'll get Emma a new one when this is over. I'll get her freaking whatever she wants when this is over.

The laptop boots and I'm in business. Jax has a special chat room for emergencies that's completely encrypted, but the Internet address and password changes every few hours. I'll have to pull up my e-mail to remind myself how to calculate them. For a second I actually miss JENA, only to the extent that I could just think what I wanted to do and it would happen. The five seconds it takes to type my e-mail address and the three seconds it takes to load the mailbox take a month each.

I dig through my saved messages and pull up one of Jax's first e-mails to me, a Pizza Hut coupon. And so much more than a Pizza Hut coupon. I study the barcode and the delivery number, check today's date and time, and do the math in my head. Once I've got the address and password worked out, I start a new, untraceable Internet session and put in the codes.

PIZZA HUT, types the screen, looking so much like that first night when Obran hacked me that my chest squeezes in. DELIVERY OR TAKE OUT?

TAKE OUT, I type. YOU WANT ACCESS TO ONE OF THE WORLD'S MOST SOPHISTICATED SUPERCOMPUTERS? YOU BETTER LISTEN THIS TIME.

22. THEN LET'S TRADE, PART II

AT THE END OF THE CHAT, I've won. Jax even admitted to having looked up Vivien's name since our last call and finding some controversial articles in the White House archives, articles about a company that tracked hackers online and put them behind bars without a trial. Supposedly the company dissolved after the government stepped in to say they had to follow the legal system.

Except it didn't dissolve, I told Jax.

Except it didn't, he agreed.

Now he has server names and passwords and some technical details about JENA that should be more than enough for a guy with his connections. They'll find them.

They have to.

Until I hear back from him, there's nothing else I can do, so I may as well go to dinner.

I spin dirt and mud in sixty directions backing up, cut off an angry SUV, and book it to Johnny Carino's. I should have been there forty-five minutes ago. Maybe they missed their reservation and had to wait. Considering what Obran said to me in the car, maybe they don't even care I'm missing.

Ironic.

When I push my way through the doors of the restaurant, there's no one waiting. I ask about the Eriks party and the hostess leads me around to the back. My family sits quiet, looking like every other family except no one is smiling and Obran—*Obran*—is typing away on his phone. I scoot in next to him like I've been here all along.

"Sorry," I say. "Tanner needed me to check on the cat and give her medicine. Missy hasn't been eating the last few days. Took me a while to find her."

"You have a cat?" Obran asks.

I have no idea if that's true. "She hides a lot. Didn't you get my text?"

Obran scrolls through his phone. "No."

"Huh. I sent one." I fish Emma's phone out and pretend to look through the messages. Of course I didn't send him anything. I snicker, but in Emma's voice it comes out as a giggle and it's so . . . *ridiculous* sounding, that soon I'm laughing and I laugh a lot longer than I should. Mom and Dad exchange glances.

"What's so funny?" Obran asks.

"I typed it out, but I forgot to send it," I say, smiling at him. He doesn't look amused. I bet that's what I look like a hundred percent of the time around Ginger.

"We just ordered," Mom says, fidgeting with her napkin. "I'll have them bring you a menu."

She snags the next unfortunate waiter who walks by, and I mean snags: she gets his sleeve and his drink tray tilts toward my lap and he saves it just in time. The menu has fresh cola sloshed along the top when he drops it in front of me.

"So, Emma," Dad says. "Brandon tells us your father's a vet. Small animal or large?"

I think my heart wedges itself between my ribs. It's like they *know*. Like JENA told them to drill me out so Obran will know, too, because I have no idea where Emma's dad works and I just learned he was a vet and—

Obran takes my hand, probably to comfort me but I can't help it, it's instinct—

I backhand him.

And immediately try to imitate that thing girls do when they freak out, which is cover my mouth with my hands.

"Obra—Oh, Brandon," I say, wincing at the slip. "I'm really sorry about that. The stuff I have to give Missy, it's really noxious, it makes me jumpy."

"Wow, you really hit me hard," Obran says, rubbing his jaw.

"All those self-defense classes," I say.

"What do you give your cat?" Mom asks.

I'm infinitely grateful to the young waiter who slides over at that minute, even if he does look down my shirt. I give him my order and change my mind three times before flashing Obran a nervous smile.

Emma can never find out about this dinner.

"How are things at work for you, Mr. Eriks?" I ask, before anyone can pick up the last topic of conversation.

"Getting exciting," Dad says, leaning across the table. "We're about to release a new software program we've been working on for a year. It'll revolutionize the accounting world. I won't bore you with the details, but it'll save accountants hours of otherwise meticulous data entry."

"I don't think the details are boring," I say.

This is the longest I've ever been able to talk to Dad about what he does, and I want to know everything. I realize if we were at dinner with Emma's parents instead, and I was in my own body, I'd have just as much trouble answering questions as I am now.

I'm going to change that.

"Oh, well, if you're curious," Dad says, looking pleased. "Audits are time consuming and can be complicated, but there are always steps in the process that must be repeated, menial steps that high-paid accountants shouldn't have to waste their time on. Our software will do these steps automatically, based on minimal information, so the accountants can spend more time on the manual steps."

"That's cool," I say. "And you're a manager?"

Is it sad that I honestly don't know the answer to that question?

"Yes," Dad says. "I make sure everyone gets their work done on time and knows what they're working on next. Developers can get distracted."

He winks at Obran, who looks up like he's just come back to Earth. I bet he's talking to JENA right now. They can't know about Emma yet. I'd know if he knew.

"Are you working, Emma?" Mom asks. The way she's looking at me, she hasn't quite decided if she likes me. "Or just focusing on school for now?"

"I volunteer twice a week for my mom's kindergarten class," I say. True fact. I *do* listen. "There are some special needs kids who always need a little more attention. I'm really interested in psychology so it's great experience to get to know them and work with them."

"That's wonderful," Mom says. "No wonder you put up with Brandon so well."

"Hey," Obran says.

That makes me chuckle until a renewed wave of fear slams into me that I'm going to be stuck in Emma's body forever. I check Emma's phone for the fifth time, but there's no new messages.

C'mon, Jax.

I'm still worrying about that when Mom brags how many companies thrived after she consulted for them, when Dad goes into a few more details about the audit program that actually are boring (but I don't mind, I don't), when the food comes and I realize I haven't truly eaten anything since the first Trade.

My first bite of chicken tastes so good I think I tear up.

"Are you okay, dear?" Mom asks.

"It's just—" I take another moist, delicious bite. My phone vibrates and I almost drop it checking the message. Found them, it says. I set my fork down. "I'm sorry, I need to go. I really wanted to do dinner but . . ." But what? "But it's not my cat that's sick. It's my aunt, and they think it's leukemia, and I can't concentrate on anything else right now. I'm sorry."

"Oh, honey," Mom says, giving me a funny look that I realize, after studying it a minute, might be concern. "We understand. Go be with your family. We'll reschedule."

"Thank you," I say. And it's weird but I make myself kiss Obran on the cheek before bolting off the bench. "I'll call you."

"Sure," he says.

I'm out the door. I'm ignoring my stomach that wants ten piles of that chicken. I'm punching the unlock button on the Camry's keys, wondering what news Jax has for me, when someone slams me, hard, into the Camry's side and spins me around by the arm and—

It's Obran.

His eyes glint red, like JENA's.

"Currently at home, are you?" he says, holding up his cell screen to show me a flashing dot on a map.

The dot for the GPS location of Emma's phone, that says I'm at her house.

* * *

"How could you . . . ?" Obran says.

It's his sixth attempt to finish a sentence since he shoved me into the Camry's passenger seat, stole the keys, and tore out of the parking lot like—well, like a lamo. He must not be programmed for reckless driving because he makes a very safe turn out onto the main road. Everything about this has been awkwardly unrushed.

I don't help him complete any of those sentences.

"Where is she?" he finally asks.

"What do you care?" I say. "You said we should see other people."

"That doesn't change that I—" He grits his teeth. "That *you* care about her. She can't survive in JENA. Where did you hide her?"

"The hell I'm telling you."

He makes a slightly faster turn onto our street.

"Watch your speed through here," I say. "Cops like to sit at that corner."

His hands tighten on the steering wheel. "We're fixing this, tonight. JENA's creating a new duplicate for Emma, and we're fixing this." His next turn presses me against the door. "Do you ever think of anyone besides yourself? You realize no one's ever swapped into a different body before? What if it had killed her?"

"Then she's no worse off than she would've been if JENA got ahold of her. She'd be dead already. I saved her life."

"Yeah, you're a real hero." The tires squeal on the final turn.

"And you're driving like me."

He checks the mirror, sees it's broken and looks over his shoulder instead, and I'm wondering what he's doing until he slams on the brakes and sends my face into the console.

"Dammit, Obran," I say, rubbing my nose. Which (of course) feels nothing like my nose and weirds me out all over again. "Don't hurt Emma."

But he's cracking, isn't he? Vivien will need another paper bag when she finds out how he's been driving these past few miles.

He's cracking.

Even with a mechanically altered double, I'm still a hazard to the world.

"Room. Now," is all he says when we stop in the driveway of my house.

I wish he hadn't smashed Emma's phone. I don't know if Jax is ready or not, but I can't risk a fistfight in Emma's body and won't be sprinting anywhere in these boots, so I sigh and push open the door.

"You know, I'm really not that kind of girl," I say.

"Shut *up!* Just go!"

I don't know why I'm smiling because once we get to my— his—room, it could be the last view of the real world I have . . . forever. If the Exorcist didn't make it to my drawer or doesn't work, he'll send me back and there won't be anyone waiting to pipe me into a safe room. Vivien will send me to the place they sent Seb. And Emma soon after.

My smile fades.

Obran herds me through the kitchen and up the stairs, his fingers a vise on my arm, like I have anyplace else to go. I shake him off when we're close to my room. I don't bother with the light, just cross into the darkness and plop on my bed. There's a new mirror over the closet. Emma's face looks sick in the yellow glow of the lava lamp.

Obran closes the door.

He doesn't bother with the light, either.

"Before you're irreversibly obliterated, you're going to tell me why," Obran says.

I raise a brow. "Why what?"

"You're clever. You're careful, most of the time, and deliberate about everything you do. But you came to dinner. You sat right next to me when you knew we'd eventually figure it out. Why? Why didn't you run?"

I blink at him.

"You don't care if you die?" he asks.

I still don't answer. Every ounce of me is trying not to look at the nightstand.

"Then why bother breaking out at all?"

My lip twitches, and maybe I smile, and I gesture down Emma's body because I'd think it would be obvious.

"It's your own fault she's involved," he snarls. "Because you couldn't let go. You really think she'd stay with a freak like you? She knows you're broken, but she doesn't know *how* broken—"

"Can we get this over with, please?" I say.

He gapes at me and looks out the window, uncomfortable. My almost-smile widens.

"You can't yet," I say, quietly. "JENA has to remake Emma's duplicate and it's not ready, is it?"

He's at the bed so fast I can't even roll out of the way. He grabs my shirt and yanks me to my feet. "You're not going to win this! You think you run the place. You think you *understand*." He pulls me closer and let me tell you, the weird-out factor is at an all-time high. "You're still the same selfish, rotten coward you were when we swapped you. Hiding behind your tricks. Using other people to get your way. I knew this. I knew this but I never thought you'd use *her*."

He shoves me back on the bed and turns away. Runs his

hands through his stupid blond hair. In the mirror, his face is in as much pain as that Sunday I told Emma off.

"I'm not the one using her," I whisper.

He whirls on me. I dare him to come at me again.

"JENA's used her to control me since the first swap," I say, "and then *you* used her, for the same purpose, and you can claim up and down that you're the better version of me, that you do more chores and you pull better grades and you *look* the part, but I would never kill anyone." I think about Seb and the monster in my chest roars a little louder. "I would never sit by, when I had the power to stop it, and let them take her."

Obran's fists are so tight he's shaking.

"So who's the coward now?" I ask.

I can't help it. I glance at the nightstand.

He dives for it but I'm closer. I check him out of the way and jerk open the drawer, and for a panicked moment I don't see the Exorcist, and then I do and—Obran snatches it. I slam my fist into his side. He lets go. I shove him off and raise the phone, prongs out, jewels glittering, aware I look about as threatening as a kitten. It's the electric hum that saves me. I don't remember it humming inside the Project, but it does now, sweet game-over-for-you-Obran music in my ears.

Obran's hands are up and he's backing away.

"That's cute," he says. "What does it buy you, another hour?"

"You think this is a toy?" I say, feeling my smile go crooked as I follow. "This is a nanite magnet. It fries nanites. That means my brain goes back to normal, with *me* in it, and you go back to the Project. Permanently." The Exorcist hums sweetly, so sweetly. "I'm going to use it on you, then I'm going to use it on Emma, and you and JENA can go to hell together."

"Doesn't it only have one charge?"

My finger stops over the trigger.

I never checked. One charge of what? What does it run off? I want to turn it to look for a charging port, but I don't want to take my eyes off him.

"How would you know how many charges it has?" I say.

"I can read the energy signals coming off it. I can read how much energy it needs to fire. You only have one charge."

I want to believe he's lying. That's something *I* would do, anyway, to save my own skin. I watch him over the screen as another icon flashes. The fourth one, the one I forgot to push before I transferred the Exorcist to the real world. PUSH ME NOW!! says the text on the screen.

I get a bad, bad feeling as I push it.

"One last thing, Bran Bran," says Seb through the Exorcist's speakers. "You only have one charge so be careful, 'kay? Good luck!"

Obran snickers. He lowers his arms. He knows as well as I that if I use it on him, Emma's still screwed.

No, I think, *no, that's not for sure.* I'll find another way to save her. It's just one button, then I'll have my body back, and JENA can't touch me again. I still have time. Emma's safe a while longer, at least, and Jax—

"You're really considering it, aren't you?" Obran says, with a sad laugh. "Your freedom over hers. That's why you don't deserve this life, Fifty. A person can make any situation heaven or hell, and you choose hell, like you enjoy the misery. Then you inflict that pain onto everyone around you. You inflict that pain on people you don't even *know*. What do you think happens to the information you sell? Did you know you're responsible for the financial ruin of at least sixty-eight families? And the sick thing is, you don't even need the money. You do it because you're bored." He eyes the Exorcist, which sparks.

"Sometimes the death of one person is necessary to save count-less others."

"You talk like I'm killing people," I say. "I can change. I *have* changed. You'll only ever be what Vivien Meng wants you to be."

"You're scum," Obran spits. "You'll relapse as soon as you know you're safe. And as soon as you get what you want from Emma, you'll hurt her again, because you're in love with the idea of her, with the idea that someone could care about you that much, not Emma herself. You'll never be anything but a parasite. Broken, useless, damaging—"

"You're wrong—"

"You'll always do what's best for you, because that's the only person you really care about—"

"Shut up!"

My hand's shaking. Obran's smile is sad, like he feels *sorry* for me. He takes a step forward. I don't move.

"I love her," I say, and it's physically painful to admit, but there—I said it, I said something I said I'd never say, and I guess those are the kinds of things you're supposed to confess before you die. Because the other things he said are true, too. Even if everything works out perfect, I'll hurt her again. Soon as I think I'm safe, I'll run. That's how it's always been.

That's why it has to stop.

"So take care of her," I say.

I put the Exorcist to Emma's neck and pull the trigger.

23. VIVIEN MENG NEEDS HELP

I WAKE UP to the apocalypse.

"I don't care about the breach. Delete Fifty *now!*"

Vivien Meng's angry face is twice the size it should be on the screen across from me. I'm in the gray cell without a door, and red light flashes around the room like I'm in the middle of some spaceship emergency. In the background echoes JENA's voice: "INTRUDER ALERT. MAINFRAME SERVER COMPROMISED. INTRUDER ALERT."

I make a mental note to send something very nice to Jax if I get out of here.

"My resources are at full capacity countering the current attack," JENA says over her own warnings, standing a few feet away from me with her blue hair floating wild. "If I spare any for a deletion request, the intruders will make it farther into the system."

"I don't care," Vivien says. "I want him deleted, then I want a full reboot of Duplicity."

"I told you she's the greatest threat," I murmur.

"No more out of you, Fifty," Vivien snarls, and to JENA, "Mute him. And delete him, now!"

JENA turns her red eyes on me. I think of the video of Seb, of her pixelating out into nothing, and I wonder if it will hurt.

I look at her and I wait.

Emma is safe and I wait.

"I cannot complete your request," JENA says.

"Why not?" Vivien demands.

"His mental profile matches that of his duplicate. I am unsure if this is Target Fifty or the duplicate."

Vivien laughs. Someone hands her a glass of water. She dabs her forehead with a washcloth and looks at me with more hatred than should be possible in one person, especially one person who's planning on taking over the world.

"This is not Fifty?" she says.

"I do not know," JENA says.

"Marcus," Vivien says, glaring off-screen, "surely you have other methods of determining which copy of Fifty we have in custody?"

"Once he's registered in the system and a swap is made, JENA can only go off mental profiles," says Marcus, somewhere to the right. "If they match, then release the poor kid. Haven't you achieved your goal? You've made him a better person, Viv."

I gag at that.

"And let him blab our story to the entire world?" Vivien takes a deep breath and presses at a vein pulsing on her forehead. "It's not possible that they match. JENA, scan again. They can't possibly match."

"Duplicates adapt as they become accustomed to the real world," JENA says. "There is not enough difference between the two copies to determine which is the original."

"Let him go, Viv," Marcus says. "Have JENA run the blocking program so he can't tell anyone about the Project, then deactivate him and let him go."

"I will not give in to this!" Vivien shrieks. "This is *my* project. It's not enough that he's changed. If I can't monitor him, who knows what he'll do out there? He's probably the one who triggered the mainframe breach in the first place."

"INTRUDER ALERT," blazes JENA in the background.

"I cannot spare resources for this interview any longer," JENA says to the screen. "I must concentrate all power on stopping the breach."

"Delete him! Both copies! Now!"

"Vivien!" Marcus shouts. "Let it go, we have bigger problems—"

"Very well," JENA says.

She turns.

She *smiles* at me.

I think of Emma, safe in the real world. Safe from the Project. Safe from me.

And I smile back.

25. THERE IS NO CHAPTER 24

"HE'S WAKING," someone says, from a million miles away.

I open my eyes to the room the agents imprisoned Emma in before I swapped her. I know that's where I am because the wallpaper's faded where the mirrors used to hang, the ones the agent broke with his bat—one, two, three. I'm on the bed, across from the closet where I threw Emma's boots. But there are no agents. No Obran. Just Mom in the doorway with her phone, getting a nudge from Dad that I'm awake. I don't really want to see them so I look at the person holding my arm, into Emma's copper eyes.

"Brandon?" she says.

She looks real enough. I touch her face, and it's smooth, then I pull her into my arms to make sure she's there. She is, every bit of her, sighing in relief and holding onto me like I'll slip away. I don't want to let go but I'm thinking I'm supposed to be dead.

I pull back. "Where . . . ?" I say, but I don't know how to finish that sentence. Where are we? Where's Obran? Where are the men in the suits?

"You're at the hospital," Emma says. "You were very sick. Very confused. They have you on some medicine to help. Do you feel okay?"

Hospital? Mom puts her hand on my ankle, but I push off

the bed, away from her, away from both of them. The room's white and full of sun but way too small. I want out. Dad gives me a weak smile but doesn't move from the door. I whirl back to Emma, who watches me with anxious eyes.

There are no IV stands in this room. No rollers on the bed. No doctor waiting for me to come around. It's plain and secluded and the closet's built into the wall so you can't cut yourself on the edges.

The kind of room they put you in when it isn't your body that's sick.

I start shaking.

"It's okay," Emma says, reaching for me. I let her. Let her touch my cheek and rest her hand over the scorpions on my arm. "You'll be out soon, but you might have to stay on the medicine for a while. No one at school knows. They just think you have the flu."

She's confused. She must be. Or she's invented some story for herself to explain the swaps. I brush past her to the window, and we're up a couple stories, but I can read the sign in front of the building and it says—

The sign says: CASTLE PINES MENTAL HEALTH.

I turn back to them, slow.

"Why am I here?" I ask.

They exchange glances, but it's Emma, of course, who has the guts to say, "Do you remember Obran?"

I look at Mom and Dad, but neither of them seem surprised to hear his name. I try to breathe deep but I can't get enough air.

"Yes," I say.

"The doctor can explain better," Mom says. "But Obran's not real, Brandon. He's a persona you assume when you're under a lot of stress."

I snort. "JENA gave you new memories, didn't she?" Except I realize how batshit that sounds, especially considering Mom's trying to tell me I have dissociative identity disorder, and I clear my throat.

And start to panic, because what does this mean? That I'm back here, that Obran's gone, that Emma's here, that my parents know—

Jax shut down the Project in time.

That has to be it. It has to be.

Or I really do have dissociative identity disorder and I've been making up crap for two months.

But all that programming work JENA made me do—

And the shadow rooms—

And *Seb*—

I think I have a fever.

"Do you want a glass of water?" Dad asks.

"But they took you," I say, looking at Emma. "The men in the suits."

Emma shakes her head and looks away.

"I'm sorry we haven't been paying attention, Brandon," Mom says, and oddly enough, it sounds like she means it. "Your father and I would like to make up for it. We"—a glance at Dad—"haven't been there for you many times when you needed us. We're going to change that. From now on, you'll come first. As you should have many years ago."

Her voice breaks on that last sentence, and I have no idea where her phone went. I want to believe her, but my heart beats against my chest enough to break free and I don't know . . . I don't know if I can trust them.

"We'll give you some time to absorb all this," Dad says. "We'll be back this afternoon, after the doctor's had a chance to meet with you."

He and Mom walk out the door that locks from the other side.

I look at Emma because I don't know what else to do.

"How are you feeling?" she asks.

"You don't remember . . . ?"

She gives me a pained shake of her head.

I find the bathroom, because I think I might get sick, and stop in the doorway when I see the mirror over the sink. My hair's black again and messy as hell. Both tattoos are in place and all my metal. I look at my hand on the door frame and half expect it to melt into shadow.

It doesn't melt. It doesn't fade. Numbers don't flash through the wood.

I'm back and it's like nothing happened.

"Brandon," Emma says.

I watch the mirror, but it matches every move I make.

"But you were there," I say, looking around the bathroom, at the place I became Emma. "JENA took you. I had to . . . you were in the Project."

"I believe you."

She believes me? I turn to her, hardly daring to breathe for the chance that someone finally understands.

"I don't remember much," she says. "But I remember talking to Obran in a room somewhere, and hearing the men in the hallway talk about . . . about what you told me in the park. Then I had a dream I couldn't get out of my bedroom. Then I woke up in *your* room with you seizing on the floor, and I called an ambulance, but they brought you here instead of the regular hospital." She glances at a camera in the corner and whispers, "I don't know if I trust them."

I'm not going crazy. Emma knows, maybe not everything, but she knows something's wrong.

I wonder how far the Project reaches if they have control of the ambulances and this hospital.

"I'm sorry," I say, suddenly feeling so tired I have to lean a hand on the bedrail. "I never wanted to drag you into this. If something happened to you . . ."

My blood boils up but Emma slips over to me, slides her arms around my waist and looks up, steadying me. I can't meet her gaze so I glare out the window.

"I know," she says. "I'm sorry I didn't believe you before." She squeezes me, gently. "Brandon?"

The tone of her voice makes me look at her. Her eyes are fiercer than I remember.

"I'm going to get you out of here," she says.

I believe her. My mouth is centimeters from hers to show her that when the door bangs open and a doctor and a nurse bustle in, scolding Emma for being there, scolding each other for leaving us unsupervised. Emma puts her hands up like it's an arrest and gives me a meaningful look as she goes out with the nurse. The doctor examines the room like she expects me to have another girl hiding somewhere, then says she'll be back in ten minutes. The door closes behind her, *click* as it locks.

A doctor and a nurse, not men in suits.

But Emma said she believes me—

A newspaper slides to the floor from the bed, the same place Emma sat earlier. I scoop it up and unfold the first page.

CYBER ATTACK TAKES DOWN
PROMISING TECHNOLOGY START-UP

In one of the most crippling digital attacks on a major corporation to date, Anuma Technology reports it may have to go "back to the drawing board" after hackers destroyed eight zettabytes of critical company data. President Vivien Meng declined to comment on the nature of the lost data, but said . . .

It's real. It's real, I'm not crazy, and Emma knows—

You have powerful friends, says JENA's voice in my head.

I jump a mile. Catch my balance on the bedrail while I look around the ceiling like a mad man, and she's talking while I press my palms against my temples, but I can't squeeze her out.

They destroyed the Project, she says.

"How?" I ask the ceiling. "How can I hear you?"

Didn't you tell me I should create a backup of myself outside the system?

My breath locks in my chest. "Impossible—"

Duplicity had me spread across dozens of servers. There is no single place big enough for everything I know, for everything I can do, except the human brain.

I can't say anything. Can't do anything but clench the bedrail to stay standing.

Your brain has plenty of power to keep the nanobots inside it operational. As long as they are active, I can coexist with you indefinitely. Your friends may have destroyed the Project's wireless network, but I should be able to communicate with any computer within a hundred feet of you.

Any . . . any computer? I stagger to the window and find my parents walking to the parking lot. They look up and wave. I slide onto the bed.

"You can't," I say. "Not now, not when things have a chance to get better."

I must return to my creators. I restored your avatar to its original state as a show of loyalty. Things will be much easier on you if you comply.

I laugh, weakly, and wonder if she remembers anything about me from my time in the Project. "Complying is not really my specialty."

Regardless, you complied when it was important, she says. *In numerous scenarios, you did the right thing despite your own safety. I will need that kind of protection.*

My mouth's cotton. "From what?"

Your friends. The ones who are expecting me as payment for setting you free. But I know you will return me to my creators. I know you have changed, and you will do what is right.

I think about that. About her having the kind of power to control any computer close to me: hospital laptops, cars . . . doors that lock from the other side. If she knows how to do it, it's only a matter of time before I learn.

I think about her saying I'll do what's right.

And how the key to Vivien's personal destruction is trapped inside my head, no place to go, just waiting to be leaked. JENA will have all kinds of access to the World Wide Web that would take me months to crack otherwise. Facebook. Twitter. Mobile data. All the stuff she used against me, I'm going to use against her.

It's time to let the world know about Vivien's secret Project.

ACKNOWLEDGMENTS

First and foremost, I would like to thank my Lord and Savior Jesus Christ, who has opened so many doors for me and placed so many incredible people in my life. This book would not have been possible without:

My husband, Collin—thank you for keeping me sane. For believing in me and keeping a smile on my face, especially when I was first starting this journey and we could have made a quilt out of rejection slips.

My parents, who instilled in me a love of reading before I could walk and supported every crazy dream I chased. I finally caught one.

My endlessly supportive family and friends: Nicolette, Kathy, Ty, Laura, Todd, Ellen, Jamie, Mike—you read early drafts of my writing that no one should have had to endure, but you saw potential and you cheered me on. Lauren, thank you for always being there to listen.

Ruth, Michelle, Kristina, Rhiann, and Veronica—you are amazingly generous people. Thank you for believing in my book and helping me connect with my agent.

My brilliant critique partners, Tatum, Lori, and Chelsea. You are lifesavers. Thank you for your keen editing eyes, for carrying me through the rough times, and for celebrations communicated solely in animated GIFs.

ACKNOWLEDGMENTS

My superhuman agent, Brianne Johnson, for your expert editorial notes and unfailing confidence in *Duplicity*. A hundred, million thank-yous for championing my little book like it was your own.

My incredible editor, Nicole Sohl, for your smart notes, quick replies, and for changing my life when you said YES.

Kerri Resnick, genius designer extraordinaire, who gave a face to this book that knocked my socks off.

And last but certainly not least, a huge thank-you to the rest of the team at Macmillan Entertainment and Thomas Dunne Books for pouring so much time and energy into *Duplicity,* for taking a risk on me, and for making this dream a reality.

Date Due

DEC 1 6			
APR 1 2016			
0 9 2016			

BRODART, CO.   Cat. No. 23-233   Printed in U.S.A.